THE MORALS

of

ABOU BEN ADHEM

David R. Locke

LITERATURE HOUSE / GREGG PRESS

Upper Saddle River, N. J.

Republished in 1969 by

LITERATURE HOUSE

an imprint of The Gregg Press

121 Pleasant Avenue

Upper Saddle River, N. J. 07458

Standard Book Number—8398-1164-0

Library of Congress Card—76-91086

Printed in United States of America

THE AMERICAN HUMORISTS

Art Buchwald, Bob Hope, Red Skelton, S. J. Perelman, and their like may serve as reminders that the "cheerful irreverence" which W. D. Howells, two generations ago, noted as a dominant characteristic of the American people has not been smothered in the passage of time. In 1960 a prominent Russian literary journal called our comic books "an infectious disease." Both in Russia and at home, Mark Twain is still the best-loved American writer; and Mickey Mouse continues to be adored in areas as remote as the hinterland of Taiwan. But there was a time when the mirthmakers of the United States were a more important element in the gross national product of entertainment than they are today. In 1888, the British critic Grant Allen gravely informed the readers of the *Fortnightly*: "Embryo Mark Twains grow in Illinois on every bush, and the raw material of *Innocents Abroad* resounds nightly, like the voice of the derringer, through every saloon in Iowa and Montana." And a half-century earlier the English reviewers of our books of humor had confidently asserted them to be "the one distinctly original product of the American mind"—"an indigenous home growth." Scholars are today in agreement that humor was one of the first vital forces in making American literature an original entity rather than a colonial adjunct of European culture.

The American Humorists Series represents an effort to display both the intrinsic qualities of the national heritage of native prose humor and the course of its development. The books are facsimile reproductions of original editions hard to come by—some of them expensive collector's items. The series includes examples of the early infiltration of the autochthonous into the stream of jocosity and satire inherited from Europe but concentrates on representative products of the outstanding practitioners. Of these the earliest in point of time are the exemplars of the Yankee "Down East" school, which began to flourish in the 1830's—and, later, provided the cartoonist Thomas Nast with the idea for Uncle Sam, the national personality in striped pants. The series follows with the chief humorists who first used the Old Southwest as setting. They were the founders of the so-called frontier humor.

The remarkable burgeoning of the genre during the Civil War period is well illustrated in the books by David R. Locke, "Bill Arp," and others who accompanied Mark Twain on the way to fame in the jesters' bandwagon. There is a volume devoted to Abraham Lincoln as jokesmith and spinner of tall tales. The wits and satirists of the Gilded Age, the Gay Nineties, and the first years of the present century round out the sequence. Included also are several works which mark the rise of Negro humor, the sort that made the minstrel show the first original contribution of the United States to the world's show business.

The value of the series to library collections in the field of American literature is obvious. And since the subjects treated in these books, often with surprising realism, are intimately involved with the political and social scene, and the Civil War, and above all possess sectional characteristics, the series is also of immense value to the historian. Moreover, quite a few of the volumes carry illustrations by the ablest cartoonists of their day, a matter of interest to the student of the graphic arts. And, finally, it should not be overlooked that the specimens of Negro humor offer more tangible evidence of the fixed stereotyping of the Afro-American mentality than do the slave narratives or the abolitionist and sociological treatises.

The American Humorists Series shows clearly that a hundred years ago the jesters had pretty well settled upon the topics that their countrymen were going to laugh at in the future—from the Washington merry-go-round to the pranks of local hillbillies. And as for the tactics of provoking the laugh, these old masters long since have demonstrated the art of titillating the risibilities. There is at times mirth of the highbrow variety in their pages: neat repartee, literary parody, Attic salt, and devastating irony. High seriousness of purpose often underlies their fun, for many of them wrote with the conviction that a column of humor was more effective than a page of editorials in bringing about reform or combating entrenched prejudices. All of the time-honored devices of the lowbrow comedians also abound: not only the sober-faced exaggeration of the tall tale, outrageous punning, and grotesque spelling, but a boisterous Homeric joy in the rough-and-tumble. There may be more beneath the surface, however, for as one of their number, J. K. Bangs, once remarked, these old humorists developed "the exuberance of feeling and a resentment of restraint that have helped to make us the free and independent people that we are." The native humor is indubitably American, for it is infused with the customs, associations, convictions, and tastes of the American people.

PROFESSOR CLARENCE GOHDES
Duke University
Durham, North Carolina

January, 1969

DAVID ROSS LOCKE

David Ross Locke was born in Vestal, New York, in 1833, the son of Nathaniel Reed Locke, a Revolutionary War soldier, and Hester (Ross) Locke. At the age of ten, he was apprenticed as a printer's devil to the Cortland, New York, *Democrat,* where he remained until 1850. His apprenticeship finished, he worked as an itinerant printer, travelling in both the North and the South. It was during these years that he encountered and learned to detest the white trash whom he was to satirize ten years later in the "Nasby Letters." In 1852 he founded the Plymouth, Ohio, *Advertiser,* and married Martha Bodine. In 1856 he started the Bucyrus, Ohio, *Journal,* to which he contributed short stories. Two meetings with Abraham Lincoln in 1858 and 1859, and the beginning of the Secessionist movement projected the young radical newspaperman into a career of political journalism which was to make him the most famous pro-Northern propagandist of the Civil War and Reconstruction Eras. In 1861 Locke assumed the editorship of the Findlay, Ohio, *Jeffersonian,* and it was in this paper that the first "Nasby Letter" appeared. The letters were collected and published as a book in 1864. In 1865, Locke visited Lincoln in Washington, and then went to Toledo, Ohio, to become Editor of the *Blade,* which he later bought. He was Editor, for a short time, of the New York *Evening Mail.* Although offered political posts by both Lincoln and Grant, Locke's only political ambition was to become an alderman of the Third Ward of Toledo, a goal which he attained in 1886. He died of tuberculosis two years later.

Locke was a prolific writer. Not only did he publish newspaper articles and the immortal "Nasby Letters," but he wrote political pamphlets, essays, a narrative poem, and two very good novels. The "Nasby Letters" made him wealthy and famous, and are in print today in several editions.

"Petroleum Vesuvius Nasby, late pastor uv the Church of the New Dispensation, Chaplain to his Excellency the President, and p. m. at Confederate x roads, Kentucky," epitomized Locke's hatred of the ignorant, bigoted, anti-democratic, cowardly Southerners—the "Copperheads," who ranted about the necessity for Negro slavery and backed up their arguments with quotations torn from the Old Testament. These Letters were admired by his friend Lincoln, who said, a month before his assassination, "For the genius to write these things, I would gladly give up my office." And Grant called Locke "the fourth arm of the service" in the Civil War. The Letters were an immediate success with the Northern public, especially after the great political cartoonist Thomas Nast began to illustrate them.

In the "Nasby Letters," Locke utilized humorous devices such as misspellings, deformed grammar, *non sequiturs,* hyperbole, and fantastic juxtaposition of ideas, in order to caricature the warped intellectual processes of the country parson who "wrote" them. In his novels, which are equally bitter in their contempt for the baser elements of society, Locke adopts a more conventional, narrative literary style, that of the omniscient author. And his target is economic greed and mismanagement instead of ignorance and racism.

Swingin' Round the Cirkle (1867) contains forty-one of the best of the "Nasby Letters," as well as a "Prefis." The collection is dedicated to President Johnson (the first), who "might hev bin Diktater." The book contains some of Nasby's particularly fulsome remarks concerning the newly emancipated slaves: "[they] hev bin in bondage so long that they're used to it." He recommends that the Southerners "tear down the nigger school houses and churches wich hev bin built here and there, and kindly take the nigger by the ear, and lead him back to his old quarters." The sarcastic caricatures of Southerners in this work are disagreeable reading, but then nobody has ever accused Locke of writing the "Nasby Letters" for the amusement of the public; of "speaking the truth laughing."

The Morals of Abou Ben Adhem (1875), which the author describes as "Eastern fruit on Western dishes," displays his remarkable versatility as a lowbrow humorist. It is free from the phonetic spellings of the "Nasby Letters." Adhem, a counterfeiter and charlatan from Maine, comes to New Jersey, where he serves up the wisdom of Persia and Egypt to simple folk in need of advice.

Upper Saddle River, N. J.   F. C. S.
May, 1969

EASTERN FRUIT ON WESTERN DISHES.

THE MORALS

OF

ABOU BEN ADHEM.

EDITED BY D. R. LOCKE

(PETROLEUM V. NASBY).

"Whatever sceptic could inquire for,
For every why he had a wherefore."

HUDIBRAS.

BOSTON:
LEE AND SHEPARD, PUBLISHERS.
NEW YORK:
LEE, SHEPARD, AND DILLINGHAM.
1875.

Electrotyped and Printed by
ALFRED MUDGE & SON, 34 SCHOOL STREET, BOSTON.

TO

My Mother-in-Law,

WHOSE DISINTERESTED SERVICES IN CARING FOR

MY WIFE

DURING SEVEN CRITICAL PERIODS,

AND LIKEWISE

CARING FOR SEVEN CHILDREN

DURING

TEETHING, MEASLES, MUMPS, SCARLATINA, AND OTHER DISEASES
INCIDENTAL TO CHILDHOOD,

RECEIVING THEREFOR

ONLY WHAT SHE ATE,

MERIT NOT ONLY PRAISE BUT ADMIRATION,

AND

WHOSE LEAVING MY HOUSE, UMBRELLA AND ALL, ALWAYS AT THE
PRECISE TIME WHEN THERE WAS NO MORE HARD WORK
TO DO, WAS CONSIDERATION ITSELF,

I DEDICATE THIS VOLUME,

AS THE LEAST THAT I CAN DO IN ACKNOWLEDGMENT,
SWEARING, HOWEVER, NEVER TO FORGET HER,

While Catnip blooms, Soothing Syrup is made,
And Reason holds its throne.

THE EDITOR.

MARCH 15, 1874.

CONTENTS.

INTRODUCTION.

Many years ago a man of sad aspect, of more than owlish solemnity, and of ponderous gravity, made his appearance in the village of — I will not give its name — in the old and honored State of New Jersey.

Many men have, at divers times, made their appearance in that same village, albeit it is remote from railroads, but never a man like this one.

He was a tall, spare man, with a pale, thoughtful face, a full beard as white as the driven snow, long white hair descending in great masses to his very shoulders, keen, piercing black eyes, which had the peculiar faculty of taking in everything in range, thin lips drawn tightly over white and shining teeth, and a sallow, hollow face that gave one the impression that the flesh that should be there had been wasted by days of denial and nights of study.

Peculiar as was the physique of this man, his outward garb was more so. He did not wear the garments of the ordinary New Jersey man; in fact, his attire was of a style totally unknown in that region. On his head he wore a voluminous turban of white, and his only other outward garment was a flowing robe of a black material that dropped to his slippered feet, confined at the waist by a plain leathern belt.

The appearance of such a figure, so clad, did, as was natural, create a positive sensation in an interior village of New Jersey. Only in moral circuses or instructive menageries had a mortal so garbed ever been seen in that vicinity.

But if his appearance was an astonishment to the people, the announcement he made concerning himself was still more so. When Jabez Pettingill, the landlord of the Eagle Hotel (at which the mysterious stranger took his abode), asked his name, he replied, —

" Abou ben Adhem."

" Aboo ben what?" was the reply of the astounded Boniface.

" Abou ben Adhem, I say. I am a Persian, a philosopher and magician. I am the possessor of secrets unknown to common men. I possess the power of prolongation of life, the secret of eternal youth, and of the transmutation of metals. I was born before Noah. I have seen the empires of the ancient world rise, fall, and decay ; I have — "

Mr. Pettingill at this point uttered a howl of consternation, and rushed to the room of his wife, who, having seen the stranger enter, was on the very crown and summit of expectant curiosity.

" Who is he ? " she demanded.

" I ain't certin," replied the puzzled landlord,

"whether it's Melchisedek or Abimelech; but — well he sez he wuz born afore Noer, and kin transmute metals."

"Jabez," returned Mrs. Pettingill, "see to it that he transmutes metal, and good metal too, afore he gits a thing to eat in this house. Sich men pay in advance, they do."

Alas for genius! Plodding dullards go on quietly on credit: only aspiring genius is required to pay in advance. Why is this? Is it because genius never stoops to matters of money? Is it because plodding has in it the elements of money-making? I do not know. There are several things that I do not know. Pay in advance! What crushing words to him who has not the wherewithal to pay. How much of genius those cruel, cruel words have mashed! Homer begged his bread, Goldsmith often suffered for food, and I — but I will not complain. This is a cold world.

The speech of the stranger had its effect, as did his subsequent action. He purchased a tract of land in a lonely locality outside the village, and erected thereon a house. This was, he said, in deference to the horrible climate; and he dwelt in it in the winter, though in the summer he lived mostly in a tent which he erected on the lawn in front.

From the beginning his movements were closely observed, and excited great surprise. The man himself, his surroundings and his methods, were all of a nature to provoke remark and comment. The curious villagers would lurk about his lonely dwelling in the night, and watch him as closely as though they had been paid for the service. Paid! Curiosity will do more than pay. Men hovered about that house rainy nights, for nothing, who could not have been induced to do anything useful at such a time for any money.

They reported that they had seen him gazing at the heavens all night, through a telescope; that he had been seen all the night long watching with great interest " a pot b'ilin' on a furnis," with other equally mysterious and startling occupations.

One man, more daring than his fellows, actually forced his way into the house, and was horrified at the array of grinning skulls and ghastly skeletons that confronted him; and in a laboratory he saw a furnace, with metal that had been melted scattered about it, and on the walls a vast variety of stuffed birds, lizards, alligators, and everything else that was horrible.

I, the editor of these pages, was the only one to whom the mysterious stranger extended anything like confidence. A lucky accident brought us together, and having been of signal service to him, he tolerated me to a certain extent. He was reticent and guarded, but I had opportunities of studying him which others had not. He invited me to his house, and in his living-room would converse with me for hours; but into his laboratory I was never permitted to go.

To my shame be it said, I once permitted my curiosity to get the better of me, and taking advantage of his absence, I did, one day, make my way into the forbidden rooms. I did not find a telescope, but I did find a pasteboard imitation of one, which to the goggle-eyed villagers answered as well. I found the skulls and skeletons to be precisely such as itinerant lecturers on phrenology and physiology use for illustration, and the "pot b'ilin' " was a crucible which bore evidence of having been frequently used. I picked up a piece of metal which looked marvellously like an imitation of the nickel five-cent piece now in circulation, from which I inferred that my Oriental friend did have some knowledge of the transmutation of metals, but that he confined his efforts to the baser and more common kinds.

Then I found packages of letters in the room that read queerly to one who was asked to believe in the Orientalism of the stranger. Many of these letters were addressed to " Zephania Scudder," and were postmarked at a village in Maine, and were signed, " Yoor distrest wife, MARIAR."

Others were from various other parties, and related to lecturing on a vast range of subjects, extending from Millerism to horse-taming ; there were letters that indicated that the party to whom they were addressed had sailed under various aliases, and had been in turn a teacher of dancing, of singing, had been a dentist, a speculator in almost everything, had edited a newspaper, had been a preacher, and, I am sorry to say, had gone from wild-cat banking to the twin business of counterfeiting.

Possibly I should have investigated to the point of concluding that his present garb and professions had been put on to conceal some pursuit not altogether lawful, had not his return put an end to my examinations, if not to my conjectures.

Another reason why I doubted his Oriental origin was his rather queer use of names. In relating his histories I observed that the names he used were only such as are found in that marvellous book, "The Arabian Nights' Tales," which book I noticed in his library. When he spoke of money, I was astonished that I had never read of such coins in my encyclopedias, and his geographical information was of a most perplexing kind.

But if he was an impostor, his imposture was a very safe one, for his auditors knew as little of Persia as he did.

But no matter who or what he was, he impressed the people with awe for a distance of twenty miles around, which is rather a wide-spread reputation. I had my opinion of him, but the people had quite another. They believed in him, and regarded him with wonder. An empty barrel looks just as full as a full one, and may pass for a full one if you keep far enough away from the bung. I had got close to the bung; they had not. The world is full of empty barrels.

But, believing in him, the villagers came to him for advice and counsel on all conceivable subjects, and he always gave it freely.

They believed all that he said of himself, because, I suppose, he said it. They admitted his claim, because he claimed it, which is the most common thing in life. Plain John Smith has no credit as plain John Smith ; but let John Smith buy a safe, and rent an office to put it in, and put up a sign, the legend whereof shall be "John Smith, Banker," and people make haste to deposit with him. They know nothing as to his responsibility or his integrity : a banker should be a man of integrity and responsibility, and as John Smith adds "Banker" to his name, they take it for granted that he has both these requisites ; and the fact that he promptly breaks up and goes to Europe with their money does not prevent Thomas Brown from doing the same thing next year. So as this singular being claimed to be Abou ben Adhem, a Persian, and a philosopher and magician as well, and by his telescope, skulls, and peculiar dress put up a sign to that effect, the people of the locality accepted it all in childlike trust.

The discourses which follow this introduction I heard with my own ears, and put upon paper afterward. The stranger preferred to have me sitting by him when he received calls of this nature.

There will be found much that is good in them, — indeed, I have myself been benefited largely by them. I found his advice, as a rule, sound, and with all that relates to the virtues and graces I have lived in strict accordance, as my neighbors will testify. And I have discovered by actual experience that real happiness can only be found in the exercise of the strictest virtue.

THE EDITOR.

SEPTEMBER 15, 1874.

MORALS OF ABOU BEN ADHEM.

I.

THE AMBITIOUS YOUNG MAN.

ABOU BEN ADHEM, the Seer of New Jersey, was sitting one morning in front of his tent, meditating, as was his wont, when a young man of prepossessing appearance and good address, but whose travel-stained habiliments bespoke a long distance travelled, appeared before him.

"Do I stand before Abou ben Adhem, the Seer, whose fame has extended even unto the northern counties, where I do dwell, and whose name all men pronounce with awe and fear and respect, and such?" asked the ingenuous youth.

"I am Abou ben Adhem," replied the original modestly. "What wouldst thou with me?"

"Mighty Abou," returned the youth, bowing three times till his nose clave the sand, as is the custom of the Orientals, "I have walked many weary miles to crave a boon."

"Speak on. The tongue of the suppliant never wags to me in vain."

"Mighty Abou, I have wasted my life thus far, selling goods in a country store; but I have a soul that loathes calico, and soars above molasses and mackerel. I WOULD BE GREAT! All things are easy to thee: put me, I pray thee, in the way to achieve fame."

"Fame! My son, you are to be pitied. Take my advice, go home to your calico and molasses, and be content. Fame is a delusion. He is happiest who knows the least and is the least known. The wise man hates himself, because he only knows what a consummate ass he is, — which is not cheerful for him. I have been powerful and mighty; I did once own the cattle on a thousand hills; I owned half the stock of the Ispahan and Cashmere Railway; I was thrice in the Legislature of my State, and enjoyed all that belonged to a legitimate Persian ambition, but it was hollow! hollow! hollow! At the time I was at the height of my grandeur I would have exchanged it all for gross ignorance; gladly would I have been an Ethiop, who is made happy by the undisputed possession of a warm fence-corner and a bottle of the strong waters of the Franks, that can be procured for a dirhem. Tell me, into what particularly thorny path does your ambition lead you? Wouldst be poet, politician, or conqueror?"

"Mighty Abou, I would be a politician. I would mix in public affairs, and leave a name to posterity."

"Posterity!" said Abou, bitterly. "Would being governor satisfy your ambition?"

"Governor! Great heavens! That's higher than my wildest hopes reach."

"Are you a young man of ordinary intelligence? Did your parents take their county newspaper?"

"Yes, great prophet."

"How many governors of New Jersey canst name to me?"

"All of them, great Sage. There's Governor Parker, who is governor now, and before him was — that is — Governor — what's his name — Governor — "

"Young man, you see what fame is. In two years you will forget the name of the present governor. It would take five volumes to write the biography of Gen. Grant at this time; in twenty years one volume will answer; in a hundred, one volume will do for all the generals of that unpleasantness, on both sides; and in three hundred, there will be a couple of lines in an encyclopedia in which Grant's name will be spelled wrong, and he will be put down as having been born in New York instead of Ohio."

Abou paused, and took a draught of sherbet.

"Listen to me, young man. You are not the first who has preferred this request, nor will you be the last. Four centuries ago a young man came to me, as you have done, and asked of me what you have asked. I determined to grant his request, for methought he would be taught only by experience. I passed my magic wand three times over his head, and his whole appearance changed; his voice became pompous, his eyes sank back into his head, his eyebrows became bushy, his lips became thick, and his abdomen increased in size. He departed and I was alone.

"Five years elapsed, and again he stood before me.

"'Mighty Abou,' said the ambitious youth, 'thy work was well done. I have been member of the council and governor of my province, and still further promotion is before me. But I am not satisfied: I see men wield with money a power which I cannot with the arts of the politician, and they seem to find in that a happiness which I cannot in my pursuits. Great Abou, make me a money-king like Dan-el-droo, or Ja-Goold, or Stoo-art, or Tomscot, or any of those mighty men.'

"Once again I waved my wand over him, saying, 'Again I grant thee thy absurd request. Go, and bother me no more.'

"And again the young man changed: his eyes turned to a cold gray; his head became narrow and long, his lips thin and bloodless, and his fingers long and constantly clasping at something.

"Five years rolled by, and the young man stood before me again.

"'Mighty Abou, I have realized all that I hoped for and more. Everything I have touched has prospered with me. I went into stock-raising: my cows took premiums at state and county fairs. I married the only child of a retired physician whose sands of life had nearly run out; and he was accommodating enough to die a month thereafter, making me his sole executor. I was elected treasurer of a life insurance company. I speculated in oil stocks, and sold out when they were 200. I bought oil lands, and my wells always flowed. I was appointed executor of no less than nine large estates, the heirs to which were all infant females. I speculated in gold and railroad stocks. I busted the Ispahan wheat operators, and am to-day counted the coming man; but —'

"'But what?' I said. 'Art not satisfied?'

"'Satisfied? Alas, no! After all, what is wealth? What are stocks and lands and tenements? Nothing. My soul yearns for something higher.'

"'What wouldst thou be? What is thy next whim?'

"'I would be famous in literature. I would write for the newspapers and magazines. I would have my name on the dead walls in big letters and in many colors. I would have the populace say, "There goes the author of — say, 'The Rival Plug Uglies.'" I would — but you know what I would.'

"Again I gratified him. I passed my wand over his head four times, — it takes one more pass to transform a man into a *littérateur* than it does for anything else, — and he went out from the presence in a seedy black coat, with an expansive forehead and dreamy eyes, and a turn-over collar, smoking a meerschaum in an abstracted manner.

"Five years rolled around, and again the young man appeared.

"'What!' said I, '*you* here again? What wouldst thou now? Three times have I granted thy wishes; three times have I given thee the means to make thyself happy, as thou supposedst. Art satisfied? dost thy yearning soul still yearn? Speak! or forever hold thy peace.'

"'Mighty Abou! I would crave something, but I know not what. I have been successful in literature, as I was in politics and money. I have made myself a name and fame. I have won distinction and worn it. My poems are pronounced sweet; my plays are acted, and draw houses; my novels are read from Greenland's icy mountains to India's coral strand, and my histories are text-books. But what of it? Each step I took I felt an inward dissatisfaction with what I left behind; my increase in knowledge was just sufficient to show me what an egregious ass I was; and if I gained a step in the appreciation of the Beautiful, the satisfaction was poisoned by the thought that there were heights I could not climb and depths I could not sound. I pined for immortality, and once methought I had attained it, and I would cease my labors and rest on my laurels. For a month I did nothing, and the public promptly forgot that there ever had been such a person. The bill-poster went blithely forth, and over the posters which had my name on them, he plastered others announcing a new name. I was buried alive. What, thought I, is fame, when it's at the mercy of a billsticker? And when in the zenith of my glory, it was gilded misery. I opened letters by the bushel, from the Lord knows who, inviting me to lecture for the benefit of the Lord knows what, and they did not enclose postage-stamps to prepay replies. I spent one half my time in sending autographs to my admirers; and the other half and all my money in sending photographs to people who have shoved them out of their albums long since to make room for the next famous man. And this is fame! Ha! ha!'

"And the young man stamped his feet, and tore several large handsful of hair from his head, which he should not have done, for severe labor and bad habits had made him nearly bald already.

"Then I spoke and said,—

"'My son, I knew in advance what would come of the favors I have granted thee. Wealth, political preferment, and literary fame are three of the most unsatisfactory styles of lunacy mankind is afflicted with. Had I been angry with you, I should have married you to an old widow with money; but I chose, rather, to let you run the several courses you selected. All men, my son, are on a road which begins with the cradle and ends with the grave. In most instances, the world would be the better were the distance between the two shorter; but I waive that. Flitting before us is a parcel of butterflies, which, observed from the youth-end of the road are gorgeous insects. We are at infinite pains and trouble to catch them, and we succeed; but alas! the getting of them knocks off the gold and crimson,

and we are disgusted at their unsatisfactory appearance. They are valueless the moment we grasp them.
I have lived something over four thousand years, and
know whereof I speak. Wealth! it is good just
as far as you can make use of it. Politics! I
never knew but one man who ever saw any good in
it; he remarked that he liked it, because, next to
counterfeiting and bigamy, — two things he doted
on, — there was in it the grandest opportunity for
developing dormant rascality. And literary fame!
My young friend, bottled moonshine is granite for
solidity beside it. Shakespeare was supposed to
be entitled to a permanent place in the memory of
man; but there are those in each generation who
write books to show that it was not Shakespeare but
some other fellow who wrote his plays and things.
And at the Shah's Theatre, the "Blak Krook" fills
it, while "Julius Cæsar" is played to thin houses.

"Then, again, the fame that men yearn after and
strive for is not satisfactory after they get it. If a
man, from love of his kind, or from a desire to do
something for his associates in misery, or from a sheer
love of his work, does a large thing, the world ap-
plauds, but such an one cares nothing for the applause.
Applause was not the motive and consequently is
not the reward.

"That eminent Switzer, Winkelried, when he rushed
upon the Austrian spears with the remark, 'Make way
for liberty!' had no idea that school-children would
declaim it all over Persia, as they have done ever
since, or he would not have done it. Winkelried

was not caring for posthumous fame : it was the Swiss
of that identical day for whom he took into his bowels
more spears than were comfortable.   Had he thought
of posterity, had he been figuring for a reputation,
and waited before making his grand rush till he could
decide upon appropriate last words which would
sound well in history, he would either have changed
his mind or lost the opportunity.   So it was with
that other Swiss, William Tell, and others whom I
could name were I so disposed.

   "' But on the other hand, look at the men who la-
bored for reputation.   Aaron Burr tried to make
fame ; Bonaparte was working for a reputation : but
they both went under and died miserably, — a warning
to all after them.   If I should desire fame I should
do a big thing, and, while I was feeling good over
it, die immediately with neatness and dispatch.

   "And I disenchanted the man by passing my
wand over his head three times in the opposite
direction.

   " Son of New Jersey, take warning by him.   Go
back to Sussex County and get into your little store
again.   Never long for fame again.   Go to singing-
schools ; play checkers with your customers ; marry
an auburn-haired young lady in book-muslin with a
blue sash about her waist ; take your county paper ;
be Squire ; have not less than ten children, half like
you and half like their mother ; and finally, when your
time comes, and the grim messenger taps you on the
shoulder, lie down like a man, and thank the Lord that
your lot was cast in New Jersey, a country from which

a man can go without a regret, perfectly sure that whatever other worlds he finds he cannot get into a worse one. Go, my son! Draw molasses and be happy."

The young man turned away sorrowfully, and Abou went in to his breakfast, remarking to me that if the publication of this conversation would keep one young man from ruining himself in Wall Street, one young man from making himself a nuisance by mixing in politics, or one young man from imagining he was a poet, he would give it to a family newspaper, for two hundred dollars. This he would do for the good of humanity, and add one more to the many obligations he had already piled upon an unappreciative world.

II.

THE FAITHLESSNESS OF WOMAN.

ABOU BEN ADHEM was bothered more by disappointed lovers than by any other class of people. Every day he was called upon to apply the
salve of wisdom to the burns inflicted by love.

One morning a young man came to him with a
pitiful story of cruel disappointment. He loved a
beautiful girl in Hackensack, who had imposed conditions upon him which, one after another, he had
fulfilled, only to behold her marry another man after
all. What should he do?

" Listen," said Abou, " to the story of my life.

" I too have loved, — I too have been disappointed."

" For a time life had no charms for me, for I lost
faith in humanity.

" My pitcher went to the well once, — it was broken, and it seemed to me that it never could be
mended.

" Life was to me an empty egg-shell.

" Some centuries ago I was a gushing youth of
twenty-two. I loved a vest of many colors, I

doted on perfumery, and a tooth-brush was my
'young man's best companion.' I do not, I cannot, inveigh against tooth-brushes, but only against
the motive for using them. It was appearance, in
my case, not cleanliness. I suffered in No. 7 boots,
when comfort and private good demanded No. 10s.
Corns now remind me of my folly. So true it is
that the excesses of our youth are merely drafts upon
our old age. I wore linen of the whitest, coats most
faultless, — I was, in short, young and a fool. Alas,
that one never discovers that he is a fool till it is too
late to avert the consequences thereof!

"Of course I was in love; no young men of the
style I have indicated are ever out of it. Love
prompted the flaming vests, the snowy linen, the
tooth-brush, and the tight boots.

"Her name was Zara. She was beautiful as an
houri and as skittish as a young colt. 'Skittish'
is not an elegant word, but it is expressive, and I use
it. In my youth I sacrificed utility to elegance:
I reverse the order in my old age. She was skittish.
She flirted with all the young men in the neighborhood.
Her father was rich, and consequently all the young
men in the neighborhood were in love with her.
They all longed to revel in her charms, and to revel
in the old gentleman's money, when Death, that hard-
hitter, should finally send him to grass. She played
her cards so skilfully that she had twenty of us, all
wearing tight boots, each fixed in the belief that he
was the favored man. Each looked upon the old
gentleman's acres with a proprietary look, and be-

came interested in his cough. I was an intimate friend of the village druggist. I took a cheerful satisfaction in looking over her father's drug account from day to day. I was melancholy only when it was running light.

" I proposed to Zara and was accepted, — that is, conditionally. She told me she loved me, but that filial love was, with her, above any other variety of the article. There was an obstacle. 'My Pa would never consent,' said she, 'to my marrying you, as poor as you are at date. Go and accumulate ducats ; return and claim me.'

" ' Wilt be faithful, wilt wait for me till I return?' said I.

" ' Faithful forever ! ' said she.

" I rushed from her presence frantically. . It was eight o'clock in the evening. I did not see Agha ben Dad ride up and dismount, just as I mounted and rode away. So closely run the threads of life.

" I tossed in my bed all night. Various schemes of lucre-gathering suggested themselves to my fevered mind. I thought of highway robbery, of patent-right business, of forgery, of life insurance, of writing for magazines, and of a dozen other quick roads to fortune, but I rejected all of them. Hindostan ! That was the correct thing. I would go to the land of gold. I would turn up shining nuggets. I would say as I pouched them, 'Zara,' and so forth.

" I read yellow-covered novels in those days. Alas that I cannot now believe that they were tales of real life !

"I packed my valise and was at the station next morning. I met Agha ben Dan also with a valise. I asked him where he was journeying. He answered me. He had tired of the farm, and his soul loathed the country store. He was for Hindostan and gold!

"Fool that I was! I told him likewise, and we agreed to go together, work together, and be partners in all things. I did know that Zara — but I anticipate.

"We started together, we were sea-sick together, we recovered together, we arrived together. We made our way to the mines, and set to work at once.

"We each noticed that a great change had come over the other. At home we had been great spendthrifts. No one had squandered the hard-earned sixpence on the quarter section of moist gingerbread, on training days, with more freedom than had Agha, and no one for the yeasty cider had paid his threepence more like a man than had I. We had been, at home, roysterers; and aged crones had wagged wisely their heads, and predicted that nothing good could come of such spendthrifts and ne'er-do-weels.

"But here it was different. Every cent was saved. We did not even buy clothing. We were not like the lilies of the field, for we did toil, and if the lilies were not arrayed better than we, they were a shabby set. A rear view of Agha's pantaloons, when he stooped over his work, was far from pleasant, and I was very like him.

"One day at noon — shall I ever forget that day? — while we were pensively eating our fried pork, I happened to ask him why he ever came to that God-forsaken country. His answer is printed on my soul as though it had been branded with an iron heated to a red heat : —

" ' *My girl would not marry me till I had made money. I am here to make it — to go back and marry her.*'

" ' Shake ! ' I replied. ' Singular, but I too am here under the same circumstances. It is a coincidence. Shake ! '

"It was more of a coincidence than I supposed. Agha took my hand fervently, remarking, —

" ' It *is* a coincidence. Let us to our labor. Let us make our pile and get out of this. Let us go back, you marry your girl, I'll marry Zara, and — '

" ' Zara ! ' shrieked I, ' Zara who ? '

" ' Why, Zara the daughter of Musteef the bellows-mender. Who else ? '

" We understood each other. From that moment we hated each other. In quest of Cupid's gold, we had jumped each other's claim. We were each prospecting on ground claimed by the other. We scowled at each other as young Persian tragedians always do when they wish to express loathing, hate, and scorn.

"I am a man quick of action. Hastily gathering up all I could lay my hands upon, I took advantage of Agha's going up the mountain after a valuable deposit we had there, to spring upon the partnership mule and hie me to Kuldud. Little cared I for gold or deposits of any kind. Zara was my gold-mine,

and to get back to her and claim the fulfilment of
her promise was my only thought.

" I hoped I had stolen a march upon him, for we
had but one mule. He, too, was a quick man. He
promptly stole another mule of a neighboring camp
and followed. We arrived together. A steamer
was just on the point of sailing. We embarked on
her.

" Twice on that horrible passage I attempted to
throw him overboard. I would have committed murder. His superior strength thwarted my kind in-
tentions. He threw me overboard, and regularly
the sailors interposed and restored me to life and
misery.

" Why did they, ah! why? Life is a mystery.
Will it ever be solved? If not, why not?

" At Ispahan we took the river boat. It burned
at Mahrout, but, woe to me! we were saved. Fate
again. Escaping the perils of the hotels there, we
made our way to Baklon, and, utterly reckless of
life, took passage on the Bulbul Road, which was
then strap-rail and given to indulging in snake-heads.
I cared naught for snake-heads. I would laugh sardonically as they would rip open the bottom of the
car, grazing my leg. They did not mash me. It was
written that I should be spared for something worse.
I was to fulfil my fate. I was doomed to drain the
cup to its dregs. We were in the same car. We
came to the station nearest our village. Springing
from the car we made our way to the livery stable.
There were two teams in, and we engaged them. We

started from the stable together.   Our driving was
furious.   The prize at the end of the race was Zara.
What cared we for horse-flesh?

"We drew near the mansion of Musteef.   It was
9 P. M.   For what was the venerable mansion so
brilliantly illuminated?   Why that array of wagons
and horses tied to the fence in front?   We sprang to
the door, our right hands grasped the knob.

"'She is mine!' hissed I.

"'She is mine!' hissed he.

"We grappled in a fierce embrace.   Down I went
as usual.   It was written that I should always go
down.   I fell against the door, bumping it open.
We lay in a death-grapple, half our bodies inside the
room.

"What did our eyes behold?

"A great company assembled.   On the floor of
the square room was a maiden in white, by her side
a young man in black, and in front of them a mufti,
who was pronouncing these words, —

"'Whom God hath joined together let no man put
asunder.'

"As we heard those words, Agha relaxed his hold
upon my throat, and, not to be outdone in generosity,
I took my hair out of his left hand.

"'She is not mine!' said he.

"'She is not mine!' said I.

"'She is not either of ours!' said we both in
chorus.

"And we added objurgations, at which she laughed.

"Need I say that the maiden in white was Zara?
3

Need I relate that the young man in black was the tax-gatherer at the village?

" Need I relate what Agha told me, that within an hour after Zara had plighted her troth to me, conditioned upon my acquiring filthy lucre, she did the same thing to him? Need I narrate how she had done the same thing with a dozen others? No! I need not.

" For a time the world looked very dark to me. I thought I was a broken man, and said, 'If I ever marry, it will be for a nurse in my old age.' It seemed to me that on the garden of my love Untruth had sown salt.

" I was despondent for an age, — that is, for four days. But by degrees the aspect of things changed. I concluded that I would not die, but that I would live, and work my way to such a height of grandeur that Zara would never cease to regret that she jilted me. In two weeks I found myself totally indifferent to her, and in a month I was rejoiced that I had escaped her; for her husband discovered that she had a tongue, and, to use an Orientalism, she made it warm for him.

" What shall you do? By the bones of the prophet, do nothing! It is one of those things that, be chesm, do themselves. Your lost love is neither the beginning nor the ending of life. Several things remain to you. She is false, and you are the victim. Very good. Nature is not going into bankruptcy. The sun will rise and set just the same; corn will grow, birds will sing, and rain will fall as before. My experience is that it's a toss-up that you are not the better off without her ; and, doubtless, it's a toss-up if she be not better off without you. Everything is right as it is, my son.

"Go about your business. Philosophy is the pill for your mental system, and labor is the tonic to follow it. These two will restore you to your normal condition. Go, my son, and be as happy as possible. Go."

III.

A PERSIAN IN THE GOVERNMENT.

ABOU BEN ADHEM was not in good humor.
Ardent summer had given place to voluptuous
autumn, which in turn had been scourged out of the
world by the fierce blasts of winter. He was always
unhappy in the winter, for he shivered, — sighing, as
he shivered, for the balmy breezes of Ispahan ; and
he had mental as well as physical troubles to contend
with. He had deposited a large sum of money in a
bank in New York, which bank had suspended, in
consequence of the strong desire of the cashier
thereof to view the antiquities of the Old World. As
the cashier had conducted the bank without consulta-
tion with, or instructions from, the directors or stockholders, the fact that he took with him, merely to bear
expenses, something over half a million of dollars,
was not to be wondered at. The bank, of course,
suspended, the directors were very sorry, but Abou's
money was *non est*. He was not in good humor.

While in this state of physical and mental discom-
fort, a man from Albany approached, bowing pro-
foundly three times.

"Mighty Abou," said he, "I am a member of the
New York Legislature."

"Away, man! Avaunt, fiend! I have no job to
put through; I have no need of votes; I have no
money to spend. I have no desire to be severe;
but, sir, whenever I see a member of a Legislature,
I promptly think that Nature is not economical.
There is a great deal of lightning wasted. Away!"

"Mighty Abou, you mistake me. I am, it is true,
a member of that Legislature; but I am an honest
man. If you will take the trouble to remember, you
will recall the fact that there were two or three such."

Abou regarded him with a long stare of painful
astonishment, ending with a prolonged whistle of
expressive incredulity.

"I am an honest member of the Legislature of the
State of New York," continued this man, "and I
desire advice and enlightenment that I may be of
some use to my fellow-men. Tell me, O Sage!
tell me, what can we do in the way of law-making
that will roll back the flood of crime that is sweep-
ing over the country? Is there no cure for it? Is
there no balm in Gilead?"

Abou regarded him closely.

"I will trust you," he said, at the conclusion of his
prolonged scrutiny. "I will believe that you are an
honest man, despite the position you are in; and I
will give you the information you desire.

"Sweet sir," continued Abou, "three centuries ago
there was a kingdom to the north of what is now
Persia, — the inhabitants of which were of the same

race with the present Persians,— in which these things
of which you complain very seldom occurred.   In
that blessed land there was no crime to speak of —
no accidents, no mistakes, no nothing.   Life there
was like a calmly-flowing river; the people lived
happily and died regretfully, disliking very much to
leave, — which is quite different here.   I helped to
organize that community.   I was the author of the
system that brought it about.   I — "

" Three centuries ago?" queried the stranger.

" Three centuries ago, — did I not say so?"

"I beg your pardon; but, O Sage antediluvian,
give me, oh give me, the system by which this most
desirable state of things was worked."

"I will.   We had in Koamud, which was the
name of the kingdom, no penitentiaries, no reform-
schools, no civil-service examinations, no Boards of
any kind, — nothing of the sort.   If the Government
wanted a postmaster, we will say, it did not go blath-
ering about qualifications or anything of that sort.
It simply posted up on the door of the vacant post-
office a printed statement of what would be required
of the postmaster.   Then the first man who said he
wanted the place was appointed."

" Were not bonds required of him?"

" No.   He took the place, and went on with his
duties."

" But suppose he proved a defaulter?"

" He was immediately caught and hanged."

" Hung for a defalcation?"

" Certainly, and for a mistake as well.   If there

was an error in his accounts, by so much as a pound
of wrapping-twine, he was hung out of hand."

"But suppose his irregularities were the result of
bad business qualities?"

"Then he was hung for being a bad business man.
What we wanted was honesty and capacity; and as
we did with postmasters, we did with everybody
else. Suppose a railroad train ran off the track, — a
coroner's jury was convened over the bodies of the
killed. Suppose they discovered the fact that a rail
was out of order, or that the road was not properly
patrolled, we hung the president, directors, and
superintendent. If the accident was caused by any
slip on the part of the conductor, he was hung; and
so on. Once we hung all the officials of the Teheran
and Ispahan Road, and from that time there were no
accidents on that line. Their successors were tolerably careful; the superintendent slept very little;
and the company hung up a miniature gallows in the
cab of every locomotive to remind the engineer of
his certain fate in the event of trouble.

"Then we carried the same rule into everything.
The people deposited with the First National Bank
of Picalilly. Very good. The bank suspended one
morning. Exactly. The authorities took the president, cashier, and board of directors all out and
hung them, because they had been guilty of suspen-
sion.

"'I did n't steal a dollar of this money,' said the
president. 'It was lost in speculating in Persian
Gulf Mail.'

"'Divil a difference,' said the judge, 'where it was lost. Ye have n't got it.'

"'But you won't hang a man who has not stolen, will you?' says the president.

"'I will hang you, my jooel, for bein' an idiot. I shall hang you for riskin' money that was not yours to risk.'

"And up he went.

"In fact, they hung them more mercilessly for being fools than for any other crime. If a man said, 'I stole it,' they felt a sort of pity for him. If he said, 'I lost it,' they felt none at all, and strung him up in a minute."

"Did they hang always for murder?"

"Certainly; all they wanted to know was that the killing took place."

"Did they never admit the plea of insanity?"

"Not any of that. If a man put in that plea, they hung him for being insane. They were wont to remark that it was not safe to have insane men running about loose with revolvers and clubs and such things, so they hung them for fear they might endanger some one else's life."

"What, pray, was the effect of this vigorous hanging on things in general?"

"Splendid. Bank officials made no mistakes in their figures and none in their business. The officers of the Government were rather careful about their accounts, for they were hung for mistakes as well as for thieving. The presidents and directors of railroads kept their tracks up, and a more watchful and careful set of men than the conductors, engineers, and switchmen you never saw. There being no plea of any kind permitted, the fact being all that was considered, there was a wholesome care used in all departments of life.

"The effect was good in another way. This system reduced the population terribly, but it made a magnificent race of men and women. You see, the vicious and the careless — which is to say, the naturally depraved and the weak-minded — were all hung, leaving only the industrious and clear-headed to live and perpetuate the species. Consequently it was a splendid people. I am, perhaps, a fair specimen. There were no lunatics, idiots, triflers, or dishonest men left to spread mischief and danger. The population was sorted and sifted."

"Is that Government still in existence?"

"Alas! no. There sprang up a class of people who got to pitying criminals. They got into a way of visiting them just before they were stretched, and sending them bouquets, and begging the governor to pardon them; they got up sympathy for them, and finally some escaped. Then the game was up. The moment there was any doubt as to the certainty of punishment, men became almost as bad as they are here. Then I left the country.

"Go to Albany, my friend, and make but one penalty — hanging — for all crimes or blunders, in public or private. True, it would entail a heavy expense on each county for a gallows; it would probably make New York one of the smallest cities, in

point of population, in the country, and in a week
you probably could n't get a quorum in the New York
Legislature ; but the ultimate effect would be splendid.
The next generation would be fifty per cent better
than this, and the improvement would go on and on
to the end of time. I have said. Leave me, for I
am weary."

And Abou went into his inner chamber and got
into bed that he might be warm. The stranger went
away sorrowful.

" The idea is good," said he to himself, " but I dare
not urge it. Were hanging the rule for crimes or
blunders, how long would my children have a
father ?"

IV.

THE VALUE OF A LIFE.

ABOU BEN ADHEM, the magician, was sitting under his own vine and fig-tree, in front of his tent, in New Jersey, one bright morning in May. He was in an admirable frame of mind. He had killed two life-insurance solicitors the day before; he had subscribed for the last book that had been put in the hands of canvassers; he had his hired man, armed with a double-barrelled shot-gun, at the gate on the main road lying for patent gate and lightning-rod men, so he had a fair prospect for a quiet day. He was musing on life, and trying to solve that great problem, wherein he was doing a most foolish thing; for life is a riddle which will solve itself, if you wait long enough. Death is the great solver.

The solution can be hastened somewhat by late suppers and whiskey, but it will come to all, sooner or later, without these or any other aids. Wise as Abou was, it never occurred to him that if there be a future he would know all about it in time; and if there should not be one, the matter would not bother him much after he had got through with the present. In dwelling on this subject, the summit of Abou's physical structure was not horizontal. But all great men have their weaknesses. The editor hereof presumes that a critical examination of himself would develop some trifling faults.

But Abou's dream of an entirely quiet day was not to be realized. He was just smoking his second pipe, when a young man, whose intellectual face was overspread with deep concern, appeared to him.

"What wouldst thou with me?" said Abou, haughtily. "Speak, man, speak!"

"Mighty Abou, I need thy help. I am dying, Egypt, dying. I have a cough which is tearing me to pieces; I have also dyspepsia, liver complaint, bronchitis, asthma, consumption, Bright's disease of the kidneys, and neuralgia, with a few other diseases too tedious to mention, and they are all growing worse daily."

"Hast tried the regular physicians?"

"I have."

"The irregulars?"

"Verily."

"The patent medicines?"

"All of them."

"The retired physician whose sands of life have nearly run out?"

"Yes."

"Then go home in peace. If you have tried all these and still live, I know of nothing that can kill you."

"But, mighty Abou, I am dying nevertheless."

"Well, why not die then, without bothering me? I am no balm in Gilead, nor am I a healing balsam. I have power, it is true — "

"Mighty Abou, I know you have, and that power exert for me. I care not to live for myself, but for my fellows. I am the leading man in my native village. I edit the weekly paper; I am mayor; I run the Church and am president of the School Board. If I should die, New Athens would go as straight to ruin as a pigeon could fly. It would not survive me."

Abou had him now. He had an opportunity to moralize, and in good square moralizing Abou was equalled by few and excelled by none. It was his best hold, and he never missed an opportunity. So he lighted a fresh pipe and went for the young man.

"My young friend, you fancy that, should you die, New Athens would go to ruin. Listen.

"Long ago, in the dim years before the flood, I was sailing on the Persian Gulf in the stanch A 1 clipper ship, the 'Mary Ann.' Suddenly there arose a terrible storm. The winds howled like an Irish riot, the lightnings flashed with a vividness which was appalling, and the thunders rolled as though the demons of the air were playing continuous games of ten-pins. It was a fearsome night. The darkness was so intense that the lights on the headlands showed not, and we were plunging through it, helpless, in the power of the tempest, on a pitiless coast. The captain — Perkins was his name — had lost his reckoning, and the 'Mary Ann,' uncontrolled and uncontrollable, was speeding on to her doom.

"Captain Perkins stood at his post calm and self-possessed. 'So long ez we hev sea-room,' said he, in his marked Afghanistan dialect, 'so long ez we hev sea-room and kin keep shet uv the pesky rocks we're all right. The 'Mary Ann' can't be swamped nohow. But this is an ugly coast. And Captain Perkins took a fresh chew of tobacco, and peered anxiously into the darkness.

"Just then the passengers began to learn of the danger they were in, and came rushing up the aft binnacle quarter-deck, in wild confusion.

"'Captain,' shrieked one, 'save the vessel! save her! I am the editor of the "Ispahan Morning Herald," which has the largest circulation of any paper in Persia. If I perish, the "Herald" perishes with me. Save me for the sake of Ispahan!'

"'Go to!' outspoke the bold captain. 'You bet I'll save the vessel — for my own sake. Be chesm, on my head be it. Rest easy.'

"'Save the ship!' shrieked another. 'I am the governor of a province. If I perish, who shall rule it? Anarchy and confusion ensue, and wide-spread woe follows. For the sake of the province save the ship!'

"'Save the ship!' shrieked a third. 'I am the president of the First National Bank of Ispahan; if I perish, down goes the bank.'

"'Save the ship!' yelled a fourth. 'I am the president of the Cashmere and Bulbul Railway Company. If I go down, who can manage that great corporation?'

"'Save the ship!' cried a fifth. 'I am president of the Everlasting, Equal Benefit, Remunerative, Life and Trust Insurance Company. Who can run that machine if I am taken?'

"And these excited Orientals howled to the captain as to the terrible consequences of their untimely taking-off to that degree that they actually impressed me. I felt that never vessel carried so much greatness, and that if it should be lost, with its passengers, Persia would be ruined.

"The vessel was lost, nevertheless. The 'Mary Ann' was on a dangerous coast, and Captain Perkins knew it, but went to his state-room to sleep. She struck, and I was the only one saved, thanks to my magic art — and a hen-coop. I swam ashore safe, but somewhat damp.

"I made my way to Ispahan, but I could not stay there. As these men had all perished, I supposed, of course, that ruin, wide-spread, would ensue. I supposed the 'Herald' would — to use a vulgarism which I detest — peg out, that the bank would (to use another) bust, that the Railroad and Insurance Company would stop, and that rebellion would break out in the provinces; so, before the news got about, I sold my property and came to New Jersey.

"My son, the moral is coming now, so wake up. I had been here six months when I got letters from Ispahan. There wasn't ruin to any alarming extent in Persia; things seemed to go on about as usual. A new governor was appointed over the province, and the province fared better than ever. There was less

plundering than before, for the new governor was
vigilant ; he refused to let the members of the pro-
vincial legislature vote themselves back-pay, and he
squelched two Credit Mobiliers. As he was rich when
he was appointed, it was not necessary for him to
steal much, and he had no relatives. The stockholders
of the 'Herald' elected a new editor, and the paper
was better than ever ; the new man was the first to in-
troduce interviewing into Ispahan, and he organized
an expedition to find Livingstone. The Railroad Company elected a new president, who put on palace and
sleeping cars, and actually made the line pay a dividend ; and as for the bank, bless you, the drowned
president was diminutive tubers compared with his
successor. He brought the concern to a smash-up in
half the time it would have taken the old one, which
enabled the stockholders to retire with fortunes in
middle life. The new life-insurance president was a
vast improvement on his predecessor. He was a man
of broad views. He devised the brilliant idea of
arming his solicitors with Derringer pistols.

"So you see, my friend, things went on the better for the drowning of these important men. Indeed, the people of Ispahan swore that if they could
be sure of so great an improvement every time, they
would like more shipwrecks ; and they got into a
habit of praying Allah for high winds every time the
dignitaries of Ispahan went out on the Gulf on an
excursion.

"Young man, go home. If your life is of any
use to yourself, save it ; but if you are trying to save

it out of regard for your fellows, spare yourself the
trouble. There were men in New Athens before
your time, and there will be after.

"When you are as old and as wise as I am, you
will know that one man is of very little account
in this world, no matter who he is. Do you doubt
this? If so, die, and as you look down, or up, as
the case may be, from your spirit-abiding place, you
will realize the humiliating fact that in a week no one
will realize that you are gone; in three weeks the
few who do remember the event will probably be
glad of it, and will be sorry you did not die sooner.
Go to, young man, go to!"

And Abou waved him off haughtily, and went in
to his dinner.

V.

THE YOUNG MAN OF CAIRO.

ABOU BEN ADHEM was approached one evening by a young man who propounded to him an unusual question.

" Great Abou, is there any such thing as everlasting constancy in woman ? "

Abou was comfortable. The night was beautiful, overhead the stars shone brightly, the air was balmy, and his chibouque was smoking freely and the tobacco suited him.

" Young man," said he, " I will answer thy interrogatory after the manner of the great and genial Lincoln, whom may Allah ever have in his keeping ! I will tell thee a story of real life.

" The scene is laid in a deep grotto in the garden of the proud merchant of Cairo, Ebn Becar. Nature had spread herself in fixing up this identical spot for a garden, and when Nature had run out of material and patience, Art stepped in and completed the job. The orange and the spruce mingled their leafy boughs, while the fragrant date, the whispering pine, the umbrageous palm, and the wide-spreading fir added to

the beauty of this Paradise in miniature. Hanging
on the boughs of these trees, the turtle-dove, the
nightingale, and the bulbul answered the lute with
which Zara, the daughter of Ebn Becar, the Wealthy,
accompanied her sweet voice. The nightingale sang
one strain and subsided into silence. ' What is my
voice to hers?' sighed the bulbul, as he sadly cut
short a roulade and listened. And the nightingale
turned green with envy as he heard her.

" But sweet as was the voice of Zara, sweeter was
her person. Peerless in beauty was she. Nature
ne'er before had made a face so sweet or a form so
fair; never, combined in one young female person,
had there been such eyes, such hair, such teeth, such
complexion, et cetera.

"' Wilt thou love me now as then?' sang she;
when a manly voice exclaimed, ' You bet!' and
Yusef Thaher, bounding from the thick foliage which
surrounded the grotto, stood before her.

"' Yusef!' exclaimed she, dropping her lute.

"' Zara!' retorted he, pressing her to his manly
bosom.

" And with their lips glued together, he drinking
in the sweetness of her breath and she drinking in
the sweetness of his breath (he had joined the Band
of Hope in his infancy, and had never used tobacco
in any form), they stood for several minutes.

" Yusef Thaher was the only son of a widow, living in the suburbs of Cairo. The mother of Yusef
was a noble dame, who had seen better days. Her
husband had been formerly an officer in the Janis-

saries, but he was n't at the time I speak of. Some
years before he had embarked in a little conspiracy
against the reigning caliph, which, being prematurely
discovered, left him short a head, and he retired from
active life to a cemetery, where he remained cool and
quiet.   His possessions were confiscated by the
caliph, as is the custom of the country ; his wife was
bastinadoed, which destroyed all of her beauty ; and
as with neither beauty nor money she could not
marry again, she drowned her sorrows in a wash-
tub, out of which vessel she extracted her daily
bread.

"Yusef resembled his lamented father to a degree
quite complimentary to the virtue of his mother.
He was a youth of genius, and consequently despised
labor ; and spent all his time, and as much of his
mother's hard-earned money as he could coax out of
her, in idling with the gay gallants of Cairo.   His
clothes were always of the latest style and of the best
material.   They were not always paid for, — in fact,
several tailors had gone into premature bankruptcy by
having too much of his patronage.   But it was ever
thus ! Genius is expensive to somebody.   At theatre
and concert, at nigger minstrels and balls, Yusef was
always to be seen, and his merry laugh was always
heard above that of his companions.   He was having
a good time.

" At a lecture of the Mercantile Library Course,
Yusef first beheld Zara.   He had reserved seat B 22,
which cost him seventy-five cents (which money his
mother had given him to buy soap with), and Zara

had the seat immediately behind him. She was struck
with the exactitude of the parting of his back hair,
and from that moment she loved madly, devotedly.
She coughed a small, faint cough, he turned, their
eyes met, and the work was done. Cupid had shot
his sharpest arrow, and two young, fresh, virgin
hearts were transfixed.

"Little did they heed that hapless lecturer. So far
as they were concerned, he might have been discussing the Kansas question, or the tariff; he might have
been reciting Thanatopsis or singing Joe Bowers:
they heard him not. Happy would the average
lyceum lecturer be, could his audiences be always
made up wholly of people affected as were they!
He would be invariably invited to return the next
winter, and the committee would not ask an abate-
ment of his fee.

"While the lecturer was droning on, through her
mind floated visions of a life-time with a man whose
back hair parted straight, and whose clothes were
always a fit. Poor dreamer! She did not realize
— youth never does — that hair turns gray and dis-
appears, that age shrinks limbs and humps backs,
that Time sets the tailor at defiance, and makes futile
his best efforts.

"He was dreaming of something more substantial.
He dwelt on her beautiful face, but his principal
thought was of ducats, and an eminently wealthy
father-in-law, stricken in years, who must shortly be
gathered to his fathers. The beautiful face was a
luxury, the rich father-in-law a necessity.

"At the close of the lecture he followed her to the street, pressing her hand on the stairs, and for fear she would escape him he hung on behind her carriage, and on its arrival at the proud ducal mansion of her father, he put down street and number in his memorandum book. Clandestine meetings took place in the garden, and love, madness, and desperation followed suit as a matter of course.

"That is how Yusef Thaher happened to be in the garden of Ebn Becar, the rich merchant of Cairo.

"'What happiness!' muttered he. 'Ah! my heart's idol, my soul's delight,' said he, speaking in the flowery style of the dreamy East, 'wilt ever love thy Yusef, eh? If cruel fate should tear thee from me, or me from thee, which it would n't make any difference, wouldst love me still the same? If I should by any unforeseen calamity be histed out of this, and should be gone ten or twenty, or forty or fifty years, and should come back old and decrepit and gray-haired, would I find my Zara here, waiting and trusting? Would I?'

"'Yusef,' said she reproachfully, 'canst doubt me? Didst never read in novels of true love? Are n't you aware that, like base-burning stoves, love never goes out? Ah, Yusef! when the stars grow dim and fade out of the heavens; when the moon sinks out of the sky, and the sun refuses to shine; when water will not run and grass not grow, then will I cease to love thee; but not till then!'

"And overcome with emotion, Zara laid off her bonnet and fainted in his arms. She was from her earliest infancy a thoughtful and prudent girl, and very careful of her clothes.

"'Zara! I doubt thee not, but swear it. Swear that through good and evil report, for time and eternity, thou art mine! Swear that you love me now, and that, with me or away from me, thou wilt love me forever!'

"'I swear!' returned Zara, 'forever and forever.'

"And they fell into each other's arms, and wept glad tears of joy down each other's backs.

"Yusef was straining her to his manly bosom, and was figuring in his mind whether he had n't better swear her again that they might again fall into each other's arms, when he was aroused from his dream by a touch upon the shoulder. He turned fiercely on the intruder, and immediately turned back, not so fiercely. It was an officer, a shoulder-strapped hireling in military clothes, who held a paper in his hands.

"'Art Yusef Thaher?' said this oppressor.

"'I am,' proudly said the youth; at which Zara, who had come to the conclusion that she had been fainting long enough, awoke with a sigh.

"'I have been searching for you, my buck, high and low,' said he. 'You're drafted, and must go where glory waits you!'

"'Wretch!' retorted Yusef, 'thou liest! The quota of our ward was made up a week ago.'

"'Ha! ha!' sneered the hireling, 'not so fast. In truth, you thought so, and faith so did I, but we want more men, and the caliph revised the figures

for a dozen of the wards, this among the others.   The
draft was drawn this morning, and you were hit.'

"'Why this haste?' said Yusef.   'Canst not wait
till thou hast the evening paper?   Perchance he will
figure again and let us out.'

"'It won't do,' said the officer,' we can't wait.   We
must have men.   Come!'

"'But I am physically unfit.   I am —'

"'I know what you are going to say.   You are
ruptured, have a cough, have varicose veins, and are
near-sighted, etc.   It won't do.   We have reduced
the causes of exemption to barely one.'

"'And that is —'

"'Death before draft.'

"'Is there no escape?'

"'Nary.   There is n't time to get substitutes, and
if there was —'

"'I have n't got the stamps, you would say, but
delicacy prevents you.   True, too true!'

"'Here!' shrieked Zara, tearing the massive jewelry from her ears and fingers, and arms and bosom,
'take these glittering gauds, and give me back my
Yusef!'

"The officer looked at them, and returned them
with a perceptible sneer on his finely-chiselled features, with the significant remark, 'Dollar store!'

"All hope was gone!

"'At least,' said Zara,'let's do the regular thing.'

"'Yusef!'

"'Zara!'

And they fell into each other's arms, mutually

assuring each other that, through weal and woe, they
would be true to each other, forever and forever.

"In the course of four minutes Yusef Thaher was
on his way to join his regiment, leaving Zara fainting
on the sward.

"Did she remain true to him? We shall see.

"One year elapsed. A gallant soldier was standing at the door of an humble cottage. 'T was Yusef.
He had returned unscathed by bullet, bayonet, or
shell. He had been in the commissary department,
and had snuffed the battle afar off.

"'Mother!' hissed he, 'tell me, Zara—'

"'Was married precisely eleven months ago, my
son, to one of the first gentlemen of Cairo, who made
a big thing out of an army contract.'

"'Married!' hissed he, through his clenched teeth,
and smiting himself twice on the forehead, 'Married!'

"'Certainly, my son,' replied the mother, wring-
ing out a shirt calmly, 'about a month after you were
drafted.'

"'Tell me, did her paternal parent on her father's
side compel her thus to sacrifice her youth and
beauty, thus to break her plighted troth, thus to go
back on herself and me?'

"'No.'

"'Did not her father speculate in pork, and get
caught on a falling market? Were not his notes going to protest, and did not this rich villain offer her
the dread alternative of her father's ruin or her
hand?'

"'Nary. She laid for him until she gobbled him.'

"'Did she never speak of me? Has she grown pale and wan, and so on?'

"'Not a wan. She's as fresh as a peach and the gayest of the gay. The bulbul sings not more sweetly nor the nightingale more frequently,' replied the old lady, putting more soap on a dirty wristband. 'She flaunts at the opera, while I wash shirts at fifty cents a dozen. Bismallah! Such is life.'

"'Destruction!' muttered Yusef. 'I will meet her. I will confront her, and taunt her with her faithlessness, and then — ' And uttering a despairing shriek he flung himself from the house.

"'There was a sound of revelry by night !' There was a ball in progress at the Spread Eagle Hotel, at which were all the *élite* and *bon ton* of Cairo. That none but the elitest of society should be there, the managers had put the tickets at twenty shillings.

"Zara was there, in the highest spirits. Her baby had been dosed with soothing syrup to keep it sleeping; and relieved of care on its account, she was rushing things. She had just finished a waltz, and was waiting, panting, while her cavalier was bringing her a goblet of water, when a manly form approached. He was clad in blue, but his features were hid by a slouched hat drawn low down, and an immense military overcoat, which he kept over his face, as Claude Melnotte does in Sir Edward Bulwer Lytton's justly celebrated play of the 'Lady of Lyons.'

" ' Zara ! ' hissed this singular figure.

" ' Who calls me by that name?' said she, drawing herself up to her full height.

" ' Zara, dost remember the garden, — the orange grove in which the bulbul sang and the fountain squirted?'

" ' Ah, sir, whoever you are, my papa has such a garden, but the fountain squirts no more. The hydraulic ram is busted!'

" ' Like my hope!' hissed Yusef, in a fierce whisper. ' That hydraulic ram the patentee warranted to endure, like your love, forever and forever. Dost remember me?' said he, seizing her by the arm, and throwing off the cloak, and striking an attitude.

" ' You! Pardon me. It strikes me as though, some time, I had seen your face somewhere; where, I can't recollect. Your name, sir?'

" She was as cool as condensed cucumber. Not an emotion was visible on her countenance.

" Yusef had supposed that coming at her in this melodramatic shape would wring her bosom; but it didn't wring. The poor wretch looked with a puzzled expression at her face, as beautiful as ever, but which had in its lines no love for him. You see, he had believed what she had said to him a year before about her love enduring forever and forever, and it rather astonished him to have her ask his name, and remark that she rather thought she had seen him, but where she could n't recollect. Besides, he was in debt and had counted on marrying her. All in all, it was a staggerer.

"He uttered one exclamation of despair.

"'Lost! lost!' he shrieked, and disgusted he left the hall precipitately. The doorkeeper offered him a check, but he hustled him aside. 'Check? Ha! ha! I 've had one to-night that 'll do me. Make way!' he cried, 'Make way!' and he rushed out of the hall. Baring his head to the wind, he rushed on and on. Pedestrians turned to see the desperate man, with madness in his eye, dart by them; the policemen would have arrested him, but he dodged them. On and on! The river-bank was gained,—the wharf-boat; two vigorous jumps achieved its deck. He turned, and shaking his clenched hand in the direction of the Spread Eagle Hotel, whose lights he could see, and the sound of whose revelry floated to him through the ague-laden air, he shrieked 'Zara! lost, lost!' with some other remarks which the reporter did n't catch, and sprang into the boiling waves. There was a splash, a gurgle, and the water ran as swiftly as before. The cat-fish caught in that vicinity were extraordinarily fat for a week. Zara lived on comfortably all her life, growing fatter and fatter as each succeeding year rolled on. Her appetite was always good.

"This, my young friend, is the end of the story, and it contains a full and explicit answer to your question. The tale will do as well for the Occident as for the Orient. I have narrated it in the Oriental style, for I cannot help hurling the flowers of Eastern imagery over the dry skeleton of instruction; but it makes no difference.

" Instead of Cairo, Egypt, make it Cairo, Illinois.

" Change Yusef Thaher to Joseph Thayer.

" Change Ebn Becar to Eben Baker.

" Change Zara to Sarah,

" And it will do just as well for New Jersey as for Egypt. It's all one; men and women are precisely the same the world over. What happened them a thousand years ago, when I was younger, is happening now, there and here.

" And sex has nothing to do with constancy. Had Zara gone away and had Yusef found a richer and fairer female on whom he could have fixed his love, he would have gone back on Zara, and she would have found him at a ball on her return, and would have been the drowned party.

"Go, my young friend. Humanity is humanity, and a precious weak article it is. Go to, I would sleep."

VI.

THE TENACITY OF LOVE.

ABOU BEN ADHEM, the wise magician, does not leave his home in New Jersey to go off to watering-places in the summer, for the reason that life is uncertain. Should death overtake him where there was anything to make life worth preserving, he thinks it would annoy him to go into the dim hereafter; hence he remains in his tent philosophizing on life, and making life entirely undesirable by giving audience to his neighbors who hunger for advice, — which, as is the custom of mankind, they go to great trouble to get, but never regard. Bothered as he is by these seekers after wisdom, he is kept continually in a frame of mind that causes him to regard Death as a rather pleasant deliverer.

One morning in May, just before the mosquitoes drive all of New Jersey in-doors, a man, dusty and travel-stained, rode up to his hospitable door. Abou was sitting outside his tent, and had been solacing himself with the Elixir of Life. With great presence of mind he put the bottle behind his chair, before it could have been observed, that expectations which

were not to be realized should not be awakened in
the mind of the stranger, and with great skill assumed
the thoughtful expression that is always seen in photographs of young ministers and lawyers.

"Great Abou," said the stranger, "I want advice."

"State your case," replied Abou, blandly. "You
have come to the right shop. Advice is my best
hold. As an adviser I am equalled by few and excelled by none."

"I have a daughter," said the stranger, "who is
passing fair. Her hair is like silk, her eyes are blue
as yon arch that bends above us; the gazelle is not
more graceful in movement; in shape — "

"Cut it short," said Abou, impatiently. "I know
all about it. I have read novels. Your girl is pretty,
I presume. I will concede it. To the point, garru-
lous man, to the point!"

"I am rich, I am a bloated aristocrat. I have
blood, and Keturah Jane, my daughter, is entitled
to mate with the highest and per-roudest. But,
great Abou, a dry-goods clerk — a nameles counter-
jumper, on a salary of $500 a year — has lifted his
presumptuous eyes to Keturah Jane — "

"And she?"

"She lowers herself to him. He has black hair
which he parts in the middle; he has a broad white
forehead, white teeth, and he wears No. 5 boots,
which are always of patent leather; he brushes his
teeth regularly, has always a white shirt-front,
and — "

"What a tiresome ass thou art!" interrupted Abou

impatiently.   " By the bones of the Prophet ! man,
dost think I know not the fellow? Be chesm, say at
once he is a village fop ; say he is a clerk in a dry-
goods store, a photographer, a dancing-master or writing teacher or that he runs a singing-school, and shall
I not know all about him? If thou sayest to me ' My
cow is a Durham,' must you go on and tell me of her
hair and horns? Mankind, O most stupid ! runs in
kinds, as do cows. Say to me of a man, ' He is a
New York ward politician,' and do I not at once know
that he has a bottle-nose, a diamond pin, a prominent abdomen, a revolver, and a broken nose on a
face which is a record of broken commandments?
Say of another, ' Lo, he is a member of Congress
and is popular with the masses,' and do I not know
he weareth a perpetual smile, and that his hand hath
two motions — one as if shaking the hand of another,
the other as if patting a baby on the head? Do
not nature and education put on all men their stamp,
which he who runs may read if he has eyes? By the
dust of my ancestors ! you tire me. He is a dry-goods
clerk.   Go on."

" Mighty Abou, I bow in the dust before thee !
Pardon the stupidity of thy obtuse slave. Truly,
wisdom cometh not with money, nor acuteness with
lands and herds. But Keturah Jane fancieth this
man, and will not wed Jenkins, whom I prefer. She
will hear of no one else but this dry-goods clerk, and
because I forbade him the house and hoisted him off
my front doorstep with the toe of my boot, and set
my dogs at him, and shot at him with a double-bar-

relled shot-gun, loaded with bird-shot, she mourneth and refuseth to be comforted."

" And the man ? "

" Like a tick sticketh he. The mosquito of our beloved New Jersey is not more persistent. Bludgeons, shot-guns, and bull-dogs have no effect upon him. He lurks about my dwelling by day, and maketh my nights hideous with serenades. Mighty Abou, he sings tenor, and knows but one song, which is ' Ever of Thee.' Eighty-two nights in succession has he sung that song under her window. Life is in consequence a burden to me."

" Listen," said Abou, lighting his pipe, and fixing the unfortunate man with his eye. " In the dim years long since fled, I, too, had a daughter. No damsel in Persia was fairer; Ispahan could boast no lovelier. Her voice was that of the bulbul, her form was as slender and graceful as the young cypress, she was as round as the apple; her eyes, by the bones of the Prophet! the sloe was not blacker, and her hair — '

"Mighty Abou, — ahem! — do not girls run in classes, as do cattle? Say she was a pretty girl, and I shall know all about her."

" Wretch! is there no difference between the description of a describer, and that of a clod like you? Go to! Am I talking, or are you? I was rich as are you. I had been in Congress twelve years and we had voted ourselves back-pay every session; we had a mighty nice slice out of the Bulbul and Cashmere Railroad, to say nothing of the dip we had in

the Ispahan Navigation Company. I was, I may
say, the Oakes Ames of Persia.

" My daughter loved and was loved by a youth of
Ispahan, who was a mere seller of shawls. He stood
in the bazaar on a small salary, with chance to
steal but little, and was therefore poor." His master,
a Jew from Cairo, paid him but four dirhems per
month, which hardly kept him in kirboshes. He
kept up style, however, by bilking his landlady
and borrowing. His capital was cheek. The im-
morality and dishonesty of the lower classes is something terrible. Baba, my daughter, loved him nevertheless. She would steal out into the garden at night
to meet him; she would go to the mosque to meet
him; and he even, once, penetrated to her chamber.

" I remonstrated with the young fellow, but to no
purpose. I desired Baba to wed with Hassan, the
rich merchant; but he was old and ugly, and she preferred the penniless young man. I pointed out to
her the probability of Hassan's dying and leaving her
a rich widow, but she was immovable.

" ' Papa,' said she, ' I will never desert Ilderim till
he deserts me, which he never will. I can die, but
what is death? It is merely a change : the body
moulders in the silent tomb; but the Spirit, the
Eternal Essence, returns to, and becomes a part of
the Supreme Entity from which it originally sprang.
Your cruelty may drive me to an immediate return to
my native heaven, but as for marrying Hassan — not
for Joe.'

" I was determined that she should not wed with

Ilderim, but did not resort to bludgeons, and double-barrelled shot-guns, and bull-dogs, and things of that unpleasant nature. Not any. I was an astute old gentleman, whose eye-teeth had been cut. I met Ilderim cordially the next day; I invited him to my house; I said to him, ' Take Baba to the minstrels and to the Young Men's Christian Association Lectures, and other places of cheerful amusement,' and I slapped him on the back and remarked that I liked young men of spirit.

"But just at that time a story got into circulation that I had been speculating in stocks; that I had been led into trouble by Jimfisque and Jagould, — two railroad financiers of that day, who could clean out an honest man in less time than it would take him to write an assignment; that I had confided in Da Neldroo; and, in short, that I was busted. And the next time that Ilderim came there were officers of the cadi in the house, who were, as he entered, appraising Baba's Steinway piano. I fell on his neck and wept, and told him I was ruined, and asked him to see if he could not get me a place as a scribe for his master, for I was now poorer than he.

"I need not dwell on this painful theme. I was surprised to observe Ilderim's vacant look, as he remarked, ' It is a queer go!' and pained to see him absent himself without even asking for Baba. And two days after I heard Baba speak of him as ' a heartless wretch,' which remark she made just after seeing him promenading gayly with Zobeide, the daughter of Zamroud, the rich candle-maker. Baba married

Hassan the next week.   Ilderim was disgusted when
he discovered that I had not lost my shekels, — that
not a dirhem had left my pouch, and that the officers
he saw in my house were my own slaves in disguise ;
and he accused Hassan and myself of having 'put it
up on him,' as he expressed it.   Possibly we did.
Mind is stronger than muscle ; the cunning dwarf
can do more than the stupid giant.   Management
will accomplish what kicks and bludgeons cannot.
Kicks never reach the seat of reason.

"Go home, fond father, go home.   Spread the
report of your failure ; get it noised about that you
have been a week in Wall Street, and see how long it
will take your dry-goods clerk to jilt Keturah Jane.
Then will Keturah Jane wed whomsoever you will.
Her head is set on matrimony and she must marry
somebody.   The moment her present young man
goes back on her (to use a phrase of the ancients)
you may nominate his successor ; for marry somebody
she will, if for no other reason than to spite the man
who jilted her.   Once set on matrimony they marry.
The flame of Hymen in a girl's bosom never goes
out, never.   Follow my advice and she will be Mrs.
Jenkins in a week.   Away, dotard, away !

And Abou ben Adhem gathered up his pipe and
bottle, and went into his tent for his siesta.

VII.

THE DISCONTENTED PEASANT.

NO philosopher or sage in any period of the world's history enjoyed a better or more wide-spread reputation than did Abou ben Adhem. From the frozen North, even beyond the Skowhegan, men came to him for counsel and aid, likewise from the sunny South and boundless West; and no worthy applicant ever went away without receiving what he came for. True, he was besieged by "dead beats" (as the Orientals in their flowery and figurative style characterize impostors); but as as he never gave anything to any one but advice, they got very little the better of him.

One bright morning in leafy June, Abou was standing in front of his tent, musing, as was his wont, upon the mutability of human affairs. He was in a comfortable arm-chair, with his feet upon a wooden bench, and the smoke of his clay pipe floated off lazily in little clouds which hung in the air a moment and then faded into the elements.

Abou always smoked a clay pipe. He was wealthy

and could have afforded a meerschaum, but he preferred the simple and inexpensive clay. He was not a bloated aristocrat and pampered son of luxury.

"How like life!" he said, as he watched the constantly ascending and constantly fading smoke-wreaths. "How like life! The cloud has an appearance of solidity at the beginning, but when we grasp it, we find we have nothing in our hands. There is a strong smell, a color, and the elements absorb it, — it is nothing. Be chesm, it is like the work of a Congressional investigating committee. Is it to be ever thus? It is a conundrum which can only be solved by the end-man of the celestial minstrels. I give it up. — How now? Who art thou, and what wouldst thou with me?"

The concluding sentence was hurled at a young man, who had approached so silently that Abou had not noticed him until he stood in front of him.

"Art thou Abou ben Adhem?" interrogated the stranger.

"So men call me," replied Abou. "Thy business?"

"Behold in me one who is dissatisfied with his lot," replied the intelligent and ingenuous youth.

"All men are so, my son," replied Abou, promptly; for he saw that the young man did not want to borrow money. "You can see such in any grocery. One wants riches, another fame; some chase one fleeting shadow, some another; but discontent is the accompanying fiend of all. We hie us to Wall Street and invest in Harlem. Harlem goes down, — we lose, and curse our fate: it goes up, we double our money, and we repine that we did not go into oil and treble it. But what wouldst thou with me? Wouldst be president, poet, or what?"

"Mighty Abou, I cannot be President, for I am not available as a nominee. I was not born in a log cabin; I did not study arithmetic by the light of a pine knot; neither did I wade ten miles through deep snow, without shoes, to borrow 'Plutarch's Lives.' I had the misfortune to be born in a good house, of parents fairly off, and was given a good education. I am not a self-made man, so you see the stump orators would be at a loss as to what to say of me. 'My name is Norval; on the Grampian Hills my father fed his flocks, — a frugal swain.' A year ago he died and left these flocks to me, — his only son. I put up a monument to his memory, and on the enduring stone his virtues did I carve. Being a truthful man, and having been well acquainted with the old gentleman, the inscription took but little space, and — but this is a digression. I shear those sheep, wash the wool, and card it into rolls, and spin it, and weave it into cloth, and of that make garments. Why all these processes? If the sheep could produce wool in the form of rolls, it would save me much trouble and labor. I could have more time to play billiards — that is to say, to improve my mind, and I could have more means to keep trot — or rather, I mean — that is — to devote to charitable works, and in short — "

"I understand you," said Abou. "Your request is a singular one. Sheep with nicely-carded rolls on their backs instead of matted wool would be a convenience. The breed would be valuable, and would take diplomas at agricultural fairs, — yes, and possibly cash premiums, if enough remained after paying purses to trotting horses. Go thy way. I grant thee thy request. Henceforth thy sheep shall grow rolls instead of plain wool. Go, my son, and be happy."

The young man sprang gayly away, and Abou filled his pipe again, and settled back again into his chair in a dreamy reverie.

A week passed by, and Abou had nigh forgotten the young man; when one morning, to his surprise, the bucolic youth made his appearance before him.

"What now?" ejaculated Abou. "Was not thy wish gratified?"

"Verily it was," replied the high-minded citizen. "When I reached my humble home in the vales of Sussex, I found my sheep with beautiful rolls on their backs; all I had to do was to cut those rolls and spin them."

"Well, then, what more wouldst thou have?"

"Great Abou," and the young man bowed three times before the great magician, "I have an improvement to suggest. If the sheep can grow wool in rolls, why not wool in yarns as well? While Nature is about it, why can't she spread herself over a trifle more ground? Think what an advantage it would be to have sheep with yarn on them, all nicely tied in hanks."

Abou put his finger to his left temple, as though he were sitting for a photograph, and thought for a moment.

"Young man, after careful consideration and mature deliberation, I have decided to grant this, thy second request. Go to thy native mountains. Thy sheep shall grow fine yarn of many colors. Go and leave me."

One week after the date of the last interview Abou was aroused from his slumbers in the morning by vociferous knocking. Looking out of his window, his affrighted eyes beheld the young man from Sussex.

"Again here!" said Abou. "Young man, thou art as importunate as a life-insurance agent, or a lightning-rod man, or a man who sells farm rights for a patent gate. I would let loose my bull-dog on thee, but for the fact that I have had him but two weeks, and alas! he is trained only to kill life-insurance solicitors. Wert thou a missionary, whose duty it was to call a sinful world to repentance, and shouldst thou be as persistent in that calling as thou art at worrying me, the enemy of mankind would throw up the sponge, and howl in baffled rage. Once for all, what wantest thou?"

"Mighty Abou, I bow in the dust before thee! All things are as easy to thee as turning jack from the bottom of the pack was to me in my unregenerate days. You ordered my sheep to grow yarn: they do it, and good yarn it is. But why stop at yarn? If they can grow yarn, why not grow cloth? Ah!

then it would be good indeed. I should but have to
strip it off, and cut it, and sew it into garments ; and
think how much labor it would save me. Mighty
Abou, grant me but this !

" Be it so," replied Abou, " but bother me no more.
Come here again at thy peril. I am chairman of
the Executive Committee of my ward, and the election
is but three weeks off. Go thy ways, cloth it is.
Git ! "

And Abou shut down the window and returned to
his slumbers, happy in the thought that he was rid of
that nuisance forever. But he was mistaken. Just
one week from date the young man turned up again,
with a front of brass and cheeks unblushing.

" Mighty Abou — "

A shoe-brush hurled with terrific force was the
answer.

Calmly dodging the missile, the young man resumed : —

" Mighty Abou — "

" Young man," said Abou impressively, " you have
no sense of delicacy — not a sense. I presume that
during my natural life I shall see you once a week.
When my last moment comes, when Azrael is wav-
ing his black pinions over me, when my friends are
weeping, and calculating mentally how my estate will
pan out, I suppose I shall be called to life for a
moment by the familiar words, ' Mighty Abou.'
Three times have I given you what you desired, but
you are here again. Well, say it, and be quick
about it."

" Mighty Abou, at thy bidding my Merinos, which I imported from Vermont, have yielded, first rolls, then yarn, then cloth. So far, so good. But the same power that made them do this can make them do more. Why stop at cloth? Why, O Abou, should they not grow — "

" What ? " shrieked Abou, bewildered at the young man's impudence.

The young man was not bewildered, or dashed, or in any way moved. He was as calm as a summer's morning. Taking Abou by the button-hole that he might not escape him, he fixed him with his eye, and proceeded, —

" Why should they not as well grow ready-made clothing, with an American watch in the vest-pocket, with a pocket-book filled with greenbacks and a plug of Cavendish tobacco handy in the trousers pocket? This is what I now want. Grant me this, and be chesm, I swear by Bismallah — "

" Away, ungrateful dog, and let me see thy face no more ! " shrieked the indignant Abou, his eyes glowing fiercely, like the head-light of a locomotive. " Three times have I granted thy absurd wishes knowing full well that it would come to this. I yielded to thy importunities solely and entirely for the purpose of teaching thee a lesson, — one that every young man must learn before he can be happy.

" Nature, wretched man, did for us, at the beginning, all that was needed, — all that our imperfect being could endure. She gave us the raw material to work on, and the ability to work on it, and then very properly let us alone. She gave us stomachs, but did not stop there. She gave us cattle, and wheat, and things of that character. I suppose she could have put up cattle ready roasted ; she might have had sirloin roasts on four legs rambling pensively on the hills, waiting to be eaten; and each stalk of wheat might have had a French roll on its head, and so on : but she knew better than that. It is our business to utilize her gifts. Nature provides corn : it is for us to convert that corn into bread and such other products as go to sustain life.

"Suppose, O miserable! for instance, that I had given you all you asked : what would you have had to do, and how would you have done it ? You would have become lazy and worthless ; you would have frequented groceries; you would have intensified your taste for intoxicating beverages; to kill time you would have resorted to faro and keno, two sinful games that will floor a man quicker than anything in this world, as I know ever since I made the last trip to Trenton, where I lost — but no matter; you would have mixed in politics and become a nuisance to yourself and a pest to your friends.

"Labor, wretched man, is Heaven's first law and its kindest. The curse of Adam was no curse at all. A busy man has not the time on his hands to contemplate himself; he never realizes what a miserable insect he is, which reflection would lead inevitably to suicide.

"Go thy way. Your sheep are, from this moment, divested of the qualities I gave them, and grow com-

mon wool again.   Shear, wash, spin, weave, cut
and sew, and be happy.   Avaunt!"

And Abou went into his tent with the remark
that it was not impossible that somewhere there
might be found a more unreasonable man, but he
doubted it.

VIII.

THE LOST MAIDEN OF ISPAHAN.

ABOU, the Sage, was discussing with me, one morning, the question of beauty. I held that a sensible woman cared nothing for beauty, but concerned herself more about the symmetry of her mind than about her face and figure.

Abou replied that this kind of talk was, to use a Persian phrase, bosh. "There is nothing," he remarked, "that a homely woman will not do to be handsome, and nothing that a handsome woman will not do to avoid becoming homely. Listen to a story of real life in Persia, which illustrates this point."

And putting his slippered feet on an easy-chair, Abou narrated as follows : —

"It was midnight in Ispahan ! A wild storm raged violently over that city, a thing which often occurs in the fall of the year. In a neat but unpretending boarding-house on a secluded street, sat, in a room on the second floor in the rear of the house, a maiden, o'er whose head had flown thirty-eight summers. Time had not touched her lightly. Her cheeks were sunken, wrinkles yawned hideously across her forehead and lurked maliciously just at the corners of her mouth; her hair was scanty and thin, the pale red contrasting unfavorably with the white skin of the scalp, which shone through pretty generally; her neck was like the swan's — not much; and her arms were skinny and her shoulders scraggy. The only handsome point about her was her teeth, and those were good. She had good taste in teeth, and bought the best she could find; they cost her forty-two dollars and a half, on which she had at different times expended twelve dollars in repairs; so they were as good as new.

"Zobeide was a high-minded seamstress; and whoever said she was handsome lied in his throat, like a base, false-hearted traitor as he was, and in his mouth likewise. She was originally homely. In her infancy she was said to have been the homeliest child in the village in which she was born; in her girlhood her vital energies were all expended in her hands and feet; and in womanhood she had grown thinner and thinner where she ought to have grown thicker and thicker, and *vice versa*, which is Latin for otherwise. In addition to these charms, she had acquired a habit of squinting, and was afflicted with a perpetual cold.

"Zobeide was sewing, which she continually did for a living; and, as she plied the needle, a bitter tear fell on the garment which she was making. Something was wrong with her. Some great grief was preying on her, some untold woe, some desire unattainable, — something ailed her. The faster she plied her needle, the faster the tears fell, — as though she was a thin pump, and her right arm the handle thereof.

"At this critical point, while her tears were flowing faster than ever, there was a terrible peal of thunder, and as she started in terror from her seat, she observed sitting in front of her, on the other side of the table — A MAN! She would have shrieked, but terror tied her tongue. How did he get there? No door had opened, and of his presence she was unaware until he had dawned on her sight. What was he there for? No human being wearing pantaloons had ever sought her presence before; and unable to solve such a staggerer, she sank back on her seat and sobbed more violent than ever.

" The mysterious intruder was a pleasant-looking, middle-aged gentleman, dressed scrupulously in black, with patent-leather boots and a white vest, and a white hat with crape on it, and a gold chain that hung over his vest, and a cane which he carried rather jauntily than otherwise. His countenance, to use a mercantile phrase, was ' fair to middling.' It was undeniably handsome, though his eye glittered cruelly, something like a frozen mill-pond in winter. Such eyes, by the way, always indicate disagreeable death under them. His lips, too thin for genuine good humor, kept wreathing themselves into a smile which had nothing in it, — such as a rattlesnake might smile as he charms a bird, or a tiger indulge in when he is satisfied he has a sure thing on the unsuspecting gentle gazelle which is approaching his lair. And had Zobeide been behind him, she would have observed that he was at great pains to keep curled up under his coat-skirt a genuine tail, with a barb on it, and that his boots were not just as they ought to be.

"'Maiden,' said he, in a gentle, winning voice, at which word she started, for that was the secret of her trouble; 'maiden, I know what grieves thee.'

"She spake not, but looked at him fixedly.

"'I know what grief consumes thee,' — and he added to himself, 'and it has n't much more to prey on except hands and feet.' 'I know why thou weepest.'

"'Speak on,' said she.

"'Thou wouldst have beauty, thou wouldst be even as other maidens are, fair to look upon; thou wouldst have thy hair as black as the raven's wing, without buying dye, which thou canst not afford at the present price of making · shirts; thou wouldst have a plump face and a general plumpness all over; thou wouldst have thy feet reduced, and the material wasted in them placed where it would show to better advantage; thou wouldst lose those freckles, which are neither useful nor ornamental; thou wouldst have youth, and gay attire to adorn thy youth, and gold galore, and silver and precious stones, et cetera.

"'Thou weepest, Zobeide, because last night, at mosque, thou sawest each maiden have her escort, and they went off two and two as the animals entered the ark; but not one looked at you, and you wended your way homeward through the rain, alone and uncared for. You would change all this. Is it not so?'

"And bending her head like a sunflower in a gale, she whispered, 'It is.'

"'Maiden,' said he, seizing her by the shoulder-bone, and fixing his eyes on her with a hungry intensity, 'I can give thee these and more.'

"'O, sir!' said she, 'whoever you are, give them to me! give them to me! But,' and a doubt crossed her mind, 'what price must I pay? What must I do to gain all these?'

"'Only sign your name. Here, maiden, is the document, sealed with a notary's seal, with a revenue stamp on it, and a place left blank for your name. See how beautifully the blank is printed! I have them done here in Ispahan, so as to have them handy where I do the most of my business. Sign, Zobeide, sign!'

"'Read it to me,' said she, 'read it to me.'

"He read it. It was an article of agreement in which he promised to give her youth, beauty, wealth, as much of those articles as she should order, on demand, for the space of ten years, in consideration of which she should, at the end of that period, become his, soul and body.

"'And who are you?' asked she, trembling, her system shaking like castanets.

"'The Devil, Zobeide, himself, in person.'

"'Avaunt!' she cried, drawing herself up to her full height, as all heroines do when they say 'Avaunt!'

"'Shall I go, and leave you here — yellow-haired, freckled, and scraggy, Zobeide?' said he, sardonically.

"She had been revelling in a dream of bliss while he had been talking, and in imagination had been all he had painted her, and the thought of going back to her old condition was too much.　She thought of the church the night before; she remembered that she had never had a beau but once, and he was a lame kobosh-maker who never came the second time, and in a fit of frenzy she exclaimed, 'I WILL SIGN!' and tried to fall, overcome with emotion, on his neck.

"'Not any of that,' said he, dodging. 'Business is business, but please don't'; and he whipped out a lancet, and tied up her arm so that she should n't bleed too much; for it always was the regular thing for such contracts to be signed in the blood of the victim, — though I don't see why red ink would n't do as well, if it was n't for the precedent,—and she signed.

"As the final curl was put to the tail of the 'e,' there was another clap of thunder, in which he seized the fatal scroll and vanished as he came, without going through any door, and leaving behind him a perceptible odor of sulphur.

"The next morning Zobeide was missing.　Quietly she packed her trunk, and bought a ticket for Teheran.

"She was never more seen in Ispahan.

"Teheran.　Zobeide was at her toilet in a luxurious mansion on the Avenue of the Faithful, which she had bought nine years and eleven months before, and was occupying.　She was n't the Zobeide we saw at the opening of this legend, not by any means.　A more beautiful female never stood before a looking-glass.　Her teeth had grown out again; her hair had

come in thicker and longer than any you see on the
labels of the Hair Restorers; her skin was as pure as
alabaster, her neck was truly like the swan's, and her
arms were rounded as they ought to be, her feet
were shrunk into 3s or 3½s; and altogether she was
allowed by good judges to be the most perfect piece
of femininity in those parts. She did n't powder,
because no powder could improve her complexion;
she did n't paint, because no paint could rival the
natural roses in her cheeks; and she did n't embellish
her figure, because there was no necessity for it.
When the Devil makes a contract of this kind, he
always fulfils his part to the letter. Lovers! she
had them by the thousand. Half of the noble youths
in Teheran were at her feet. They sighed for the
possession of her matchless charms; they sighed for
her wealth, with which to go into the oil business:
but to all of which she turned a deaf ear. Her
motto was " Excelsior," and she was waiting for some
noble Lord, some Grand Duke, or some Princely
Potentate or Power, to fall at her feet. And besides,
she had grown capricious and wayward, and it was a
source of serene pleasure to her to have them dang-
ling after her.

" One night Zobeide stood at her toilet preparing
herself for a gay assemblage, at which she was sure
to be the admired of all admirers. She was just putting the last touch to herself, and was admiring the
effect in the mirror, when, horror! there was another
face beside hers in the glass! She shrieked, for it
was the identical face which she had stood before

ten years before, in her desolate chamber in Ispahan.

"'Zobeide,' said he, 'I have come for thee. Didst
think, Zobeide, when thou left Ispahan, that I could
never find time to come here after thee? Foolish
girl! Know that two thirds of the inhabitants of
that city COME TO ME of their own accord! Here is
the contract, but' — a frown o'erspread his countenance — 'I am mistaken in the date. Thou hast yet
a month before thou fallest due. Never mind,' said he
to himself, 'the time is n't wasted. I never yet failed
to make a trip to Teheran pay. I shall be here again
in a month. Be ready.'

"Zobeide went to the party, nevertheless, and was
the gayest of the gay. Ah! could those who envied
her hair have known by what means she became possessed of it! Could those who noticed the heaving of
her bosom have known how heavy the heart she was carrying underneath it! But they did n't. They never do.

"That night was one of unmixed agony. She
paced the floor till the dawning of the day, and wept
and tore her hair, and tore her hair and wept. Was
there no way to escape him? Could she not outwit
him? Was there no flaw in the contract? Were
such contracts binding under the laws of Persia? To
all these questions she got no answer, and finally, in
her despair, she went to the mufti of the mosque in
which she had been sleeping ever since she had been
in Teheran, as all people do when the Devil gets after
them. She told him her story, weeping till the carpet was soaked.

"'Zobeide,' said he to her tenderly, as is the custom of ministers when they are giving advice to young and prepossessing females, 'thou didst foolishly. What are the transitory things of life? What are beauty, wealth, and such, if thou canst not enjoy them forever?'

"'True, father,' said she, 'but I've had a good time of it for ten years. You cannot appreciate my situation. Owing to your sex, you never *can* be a scraggy female, yellow-haired and freckled, and running mostly to hands and feet. If you had been such, you would have done as I did.'

"'Zobeide, one way remains, and only one. When the arch-fiend cometh, give him back all that he gavest thee; tell him to restore thee to thy normal ugliness, and the contract is at an end.'

"'But what shall I do then?'

"'If you are too ugly to move in good society, turn reformer, my child, and go to lecturing on woman's rights. Why didn't you think of that before?'

"And she took his advice. Precisely as the clock struck twelve, on the night of the thirty-first of the twelfth month of the tenth year (she was in her chamber), before her stood her visitor, — this time without his coat and hat and gentlemanly attire. When the Devil makes a bargain, he always appears fixed up; when he comes for his pay, he is not such a pleasant-looking individual. I learned that once in a fit of delirium tremens, caused by being a candidate for a county office.

"'Avaunt!' said Zobeide, 'I rue the bargain. I will not go!'

"'My dear,' retorted he, 'it's too late. You can't back out. Here! See! Here is the contract duly signed and sealed, and the stamps sufficient. My dear, you *must* go!'

"'Place me,' shrieked she, 'as you found me. Take back this wealth, this beauty, this hair, these teeth, and give me back my old set, which was as good as new. I WILL NOT GO! Our arrangement is at an end.'

"'Zobeide,' said he, smiling sardonically, and fixing on her a wicked eye, 'look at this! Ha! ha!'

"And he held before her a photograph which had been taken ten years ago, and which she thought she had destroyed. There was the yellow hair, the wrinkles, the freckles, the skinny neck, the hands, and the feet which even hoops were insufficient to hide; and as her eyes were glued on it, the Devil smiled still more sardonically.

"'Would you be again like this, and be again beneath the notice of a lame kobosh-maker?' said he.

"'Never!' shrieked she, 'take me!' and she fell fainting into his arms.

"When the servants came up the next morning at 11 A. M., to awaken their mistress, she was n't there. There was, however, a strong odor of brimstone pervading the apartment, which completely overpowered the Night-Blooming Cereus which stood open on her table. The servants helped themselves to her clothes and jewelry, and all of them married well and had

large families. The house was sold for taxes, as is
the custom of the city, and was finally converted
into a boarding-house.

" My friend, there are several morals to be drawn
from this legend, the principal one of which is, that
the unquenchable desire for being handsome and rich
is what generally sends women to the Devil; and so
long as men are idiotic enough to hold beauty,
which can only endure a few years, superior in value
to other qualities which are eternal, I cannot say that
I blame them.   Every Gill must have her Jack,
and the Gills all desire that which has most power
over the Jacks.   So far, beauty has done the trick,
and therefore they want beauty.

" But I am tired.   I will lie me down."

And the Sage went into his tent and laid him down
on his divan.

IX.

THE INUTILITY OF TRUTH.

ABOU BEN ADHEM was not in good humor. He was away from his home, and missed sadly the comforts and conveniences of his tent. He took with him the editor of these pages, that in genial companionship he might mitigate the suffering that to him always accompanied change, but he was not happy. He was out of his place, and was therefore as uncomfortable as a faro-dealer would be in a prayer-meeting, a member of Congress at a reform convention, or a lobster in hot water. The dweller in Fifth Avenue, used to the conveniences of modern civilization, would not be comfortable in the simple tent of the Persian sage; so, likewise, the Persian sage was not comfortable in the gorgeous room which he was occupying in a hotel at Trenton. When the heat became insupportable, he could not lift the bottom of the cloth of his tent and get a free circulation of air; at Trenton he had to depend on a raised window.

"They talk of improvements," said Abou to himself, as he hung panting out of the aperture, gasping for breath.   " Has the world made progress? Is this hole better than all out-of-doors ? "

It was while he was thus musing, in an irritable frame of mind, that a stranger entered, which interruption, of all things in the world, was precisely what Abou did not want.

" What is the matter with you, my buck ? " said Abou, unconsciously dropping into the fervid Oriental style of expression.

" Mighty Abou," said the stranger, " I would confer with you. I would be perfect. I would live close to truth. I would so train my mind that truth should ever be in it — my tongue, that it should ever utter it. This is what I yearn for, — truth.

" Young man," replied Abou, impressively, " to remark that you are an ass would be a very mild statement of your condition. But I will waste a little time on you. Listen.

" In the years gone never to return, I was a young man in Ispahan. I was the son of loving parents, who sent me to the school of Blohard, the perfectionist, to be instructed in morals. Blohard held and taught as a first principle, that truth, absolute and undeviating, should govern all men; and that under no circumstances could it be safely disregarded. I believed him, and went out into the world to practise his teachings.

" I had a maiden aunt, who had property to which it was expected I would be heir, and my parents had particularly instructed me to show her deference and honor. Woe is me that I ever saw Blohard, whom may seven thousand fiends torment! I was at her house just after I had received this lesson from that prince of quacks. Everything was propitious for me. She was seventy-one, and had a cough which was tearing her to pieces; and to make it absolutely certain that she could not long survive, she had three physicians in attendance upon her. As her will was made, leaving all her estate to me, the song of the bulbul was not more agreeable to my ear than that cough; and the three physicians were more pleasant to my eye than a vision of Paradise.

"On the morning in question, I found her absorbed in the fashion-plates of the Lady's Magazine of that period. My son, here is a fact thrown in gratis, — no woman ever gets beyond fashion-plates. It is a provision of nature that a fashion-plate delights the feminine mind so long as it is incased in the feminine body. My aunt was reclining on a sofa and arrayed gorgeously. She had on a pink mauve poplin, berage moire antique, cut bias down the back, with heart-shaped bodice, low in the neck, and with short sleeves trimmed with asbestos lace. It was a dress appropriate for a young lady of fifteen with flesh on her shoulders.

"'Abou,' said she, with a death's-head grin and a paralytic shake of the head, 'doth not this dress accord with my style of beauty?'

"I was about to reply like a man of the world, when the precept of Blohard (whom may fire consume!) occurred to me.

"'I am sure it does not, aunt!' I replied. 'You are too fearfully old and ugly for such a gay dress. The beauty of the apparel calls unnecessary attention to your general ghastliness; you are too bony for such dry-goods, and the cut thereof adds to your horrible boneiness instead of hiding it. A skeleton, no matter how perfect a skeleton it may be, should never be dressed low in the neck; for shoulder-blades, when they seem to be forcing their way through saffron-colored skin, are never pleasant to look upon. Now, aunt, in all candor, I would suggest that instead of dressing yourself so absurdly in lace, you swathe your shrivelled remains in flannels, thus compelling art to furnish what nature has denied, — a sufficient covering for your bones. It is absurd for a hideous old virgin like yourself to ape the style of a girl of fifteen. Go to, vain old woman! Instead of indulging in such vanities, prepare for Death, who stands waiting for you.'

"The old lady did not appreciate my truthfulness. She flew at me like an attenuated tigress, and called me a fool and a beast, and ordered me out of her house. The excitement was so great that she fell into a fit of coughing which killed her. She lived, however, long enough to alter her will, leaving every dirhem of her estate to the Society for the Conversion of the French to Mohammedanism. I never saw a kopeck of it.

"This was somewhat discouraging, but I determined to persevere. Blohard had dwelt so strongly on the necessity of absolute truth that I could not

think of going back on it. So I gritted my teeth
and waded in.

"I had an uncle, a very rich man, who was afflicted
with poetry. He was troubled with the idea that he
was a poet, and spent the bulk of his time hacking
away at his verses. He had finished a poem of thirty-
six cantos, and he invited me to hear it.

"'My son,' said he, 'I have confidence in your
taste and judgment. Now, I am going to show this
poem to you, and shall abide your judgment. If
you say it is good, I shall so esteem it, and publish
it; if you say bad, I shall accept the decision, and
burn it.'

"'Fire away!' I answered, in the Oriental style,
which is more fervid than your form of utterance in
this deliberate and unimpassioned West.

"The old gentleman read, and read, and read. I
struggled manfully to keep awake, and succeeded.
When he got through he paused.

"'Your honest judgment, my son.'

"I determined to give an honest opinion, but I
said to myself, I will draw it mild. I will not hurt
the old gentleman's feelings. I will treat him tenderly.

"'Uncle,' said I, 'the poem may have merits, but
I fail to discover them. It is defective in rhythm,
utterly and entirely devoid of sentiment, and atro-
cious in design. A more stupid, senseless performance I was never bored with. It is hog-wash. It
is idiocy — it is deliberate idiocy. It was conceived
in weakness and brought forth in inanity. I would,

for your sake, that I could call it lunacy ; but it lacks the strength and fire that an overturned intellect would have given it. I cannot say lunacy in connection with it, for to say lunacy presupposes intellect, of which this performance gives no token. It is drool. It is drivel. For the sake of your family, do not publish it.'

"I did not expect this criticism to produce the effect it did, for it was entirely honest and just. But it did not strike the old gentleman at all pleasantly. He glared at me a moment fiercely, and raising a chair, felled me to the floor. He kicked me out of the house, protesting the while that a more insulting dog than I was did not dwell in Ispahan.

"He did publish the poem, however, but the public of Ispahan sustained my criticism. The wits of Ispahan and Teheran made him their butt for weeks. But when he died, he left me, who should have been his heir, a bound copy of the accursed trash.

"I followed up this thing for a year. I told an orator that his peroration was bosh and his entire speech was clap-trap. I told a dervish that his whirling and howling were only half as good as they had been a year before. In the most candid manner, I informed an actor who had invited me to witness and criticise his performance, that he was the worst I ever saw. In short, in that year I made an enemy of every man, woman, and child in Ispahan ; and what grieved me was, that in all that time I held closely to the truth, never deviating from it a hair's-breadth.

" And finally I came to blows with Blohard himself. He asked my candid opinion of a lecture he had delivered, and I told him what I thought, as he had instructed me. I merely remarked that the badness of the thought was only equalled by the badness of the execution, and that both together were exceeded by the badness of the delivery. Instead of thanking me, he flew into a rage.

" My son, truth is not the highest wisdom in ordinary hands, but silence is. Only very rich men can afford to spread truth about recklessly. Truth is too precious for every-day use. When a rich man says, ' I am a plain, blunt man, and am used to speaking the simple truth ; I call things by their right names, I do,' — set him down as a disagreeable old brute, who goes about making people uncomfortable, because he can do it safely. When a poor man says the same, set him down as a fool. I do not advise lying, but beware of too free use of the truth. It needs to be handled judiciously. Were the world perfect, — were everybody as free from weakness as, for instance, myself, — it would answer, for truth would then be pleasant ; but as it is, beware of it.

" Silence, my ingenuous friend, is your best hold. Silence will conceal the fact that you are an inferior being, and will offend nobody.

" Let silence be your rule — speech the exception. Then shall you prosper and be counted as one of the wise. But leave me now, for I would rest."

And Abou, after the manner of the Eastern sages, mixed him in a tumbler the strong waters of the

Giaour with lemon and sugar and a very little water
(for the water of Trenton is not healthful), and swal-
lowed it, saying, " Be chesm, but it is good.   It
warms the midriff and makes one charitable.   For an
excuse to repeat, I would be willing, almost, to heave
out another chunk of wisdom."

And with this Oriental ejaculation, he clambered
into his bed.

X.

THE SHADOWY NATURE OF FAME.

A BOU BEN ADHEM was called upon one morning in the last moon by a young man of nineteen,
who had walked all the way from Sussex County to
consult him.

Abou was not in the humor to shed wisdom, for
he had been disappointed. He had been trying the
experiment of transmuting metals, hoping to arrive
at the secret of manufacturing gold. He had the
required ingredients in the crucible, he had repeated
the magic formula, and at the critical moment, when
the star Xermes was entering the remote apex of the
sublunar constellation Capsicum, he had dropped
into the seething metals the required ounce of virgin
gold.

For the sake of effect he had used for this purpose
the head of a cane, which had been presented to him
by a certain corporation, for his services in lobbying
through the Legislature a most villanous fraud in
which it was interested. He could have used other
gold, but he thought the effect would be better to
use this. He wanted to see a picture of himself in

the illustrated papers, breaking off this gold head, with an account of how he had spent all his means to carry on the experiments, until finally, just at the threshold of success, he had to have an ounce of gold. Where was he to get it? Ha! There was the cane! True, it was a valued memento, but, in the interest of science, it must go! That was his idea.

To his surprise the result was not gold, and he wondered at it till he investigated. Then he discovered that the head of that cane was nothing but Milton gold, and that the whole affair had been bought at a dollar store. Then did Abou inveigh against the frauds and deceptions of a wicked world.

Abou looked up and saw the young man, and knew his errand at once. He had a broad, white forehead, a turn-over collar, and wore his hair long in ringlets.

" Well," said the magician, with an unusual degree of acerbity, " what wouldst thou with me ? "

" Mighty Abou," replied the youth, prostrating himself three times, " my name is James Parkinson Peters. My first business is to offer, as a tribute to your genius, — which is only equalled by your goodness, — this package of the distilled product of the New Jersey orchard."

Abou unrolled it, smelled it, and remarking to himself, " Apple-jack," said, —

" I accept it in the spirit in which it is tendered. Dear to the heart of the sage are the words of approval of young men of taste ; dearer is the distilled juice of the apple — when it is old and mellow. But what

else dost come for? What says Hafiz, the Seer of
Sangamon County? 'He who comes full-handed
expects to go away fuller-handed.' Be modest in your
asking, young man, lest I repent me of taking your
nectar. Drive on your cart, gentle youth."

"Mighty Abou, tell me, ah! tell me, is there any
such thing as winning a name that will echo down the
ages?"

"Echo down the what?"

"Down the ages, which is to say, Is there such a
thing as imperishable fame?"

"Young man, I understand you. You hanker for
immortality; you would have the name of J. Parkinson Peters remembered to the end of time, as it
were. Is that the desire that is consuming you?"

"Mighty Abou, it is."

"J. Parkinson Peters, a more asinine thought
never entered an idiot's head; but we all have it at
some period of our respective lives. I know of but
one cure for it, and this fortunately I have about my
person. Here, J. P. P., is a brick. That brick is
from Egypt and is only perhaps five thousand years
old. You see those characters? You can't read
them — I can. That brick has on it a record of
the kings of the old Memphian monarchy which
preceded the Ptolemies. Those Memphian monarchs
were no small potatoes. In the art of scooping other
nations they were equalled by few and excelled by
none. Their names filled the world in their day, and
every monarch of them died supposing his name
would go echoing down the ages. Now, you are a

young man of ordinary intelligence. Well, did you
ever hear of Wunpare? He was the first of them.
No! Well, he had armies, and generals, and commis-
saries, and was actually a great king. He gave battle
to Toopare and was beaten. Toopare was in turn
beaten by Threeze, who was ignominiously routed by
Strate, who succumbed in turn to Phlush, who was
beaten by Acephull, who held on a little while, lay-
ing out Forephlush and Threjax, only to meet his
doom at the hands of Foreuvakind, who in turn was
made a cold corpse by Stratephlush.

"Now, my young friend, the great Stratephlush,
being the best of them all, was sure of his immortality, and he really believed that future ages would
celerbate his deeds in prose and verse ; and the egregious ass built a pyramid or two to perpetuate his
name.

"Where now, O idiot ! is Stratephlush and his memory? A few sages like myself, who know all things,
know the name, but no more ; and only such of us
as can decipher cuneiform writing.   Practically the
great conqueror Stratephlush is no more known than
is the tailor who made the breeches in which he went
forth to do battle. He made history, and what is it ?
A line in a dull book, and a brick ! Even we sages
cannot come at the time of his reign into a thousand
years. He lived, fought, ruled, and died. He went
to death with philanthropists, tailors, dentists, lightning-rod men, reformers, life-insurance agents, mis-
sionaries, cabinet officers, prostitutes, explorers, advertising agents, preachers, auctioneers, and lectur-

ers. The cold waters of oblivion cover them all.
Stratephlush is no more remembered than is the Ben
Butler of his Congress, and neither of them are any
better known than are the people they swindled.
The skull of Stratephlush and that of his shoemaker
cannot to-day be distinguished. We thought we had
Stratephlush's skull, but it turned out afterward that
it was a woman's skull, which was determined by the
filling in the teeth. Imagine the feelings of the ghost
of Stratephlush when he saw the *savans* worshipping
a woman's skull supposing it to be his !

" As it was with the ancients, so will it be with the
moderns. The Brobinding nag of to-day will be the
Liliputian of the next century. I do not suppose
that even my name will live forever.

" My son, all this that you are hankering after is a
delusion and snare ; but life is not barren for all that.
I believe there is a future (as everybody does), for
the reason that I hold this life to be altogether too
short to reward me for my virtues, and that an eternity is not too long to punish my enemies. I make
this life of use in getting up my moral muscle. I am
in training in this world to make as respectable a
ghost as possible in the next. But I am not going
for fame to any extent, nor do I care about being
noted. I leave that for showmen and patent medicine men. I indulge in no visions of monuments
and vanities of that nature. I would n't give a brass
sequin for all the stone that could be piled up to com-
memorate my virtues. If a grateful people want to
build a monument for me, after I am gone, let them

come to me now, and say so, and I will discount the cost of it twenty-five per cent for cash in hand.   I can use the shekels now : after I am gone they will never do me a particle of good.   The statue will not be like me, and if it is I shall not have the ability to thank them.

" Go home, young man, go home.   Go about your legitimate vocation, whatever it may be, and stick by it.   Live right along, take all the comfort you can, be as happy as possible, and when you die, count it as certain that, so far as this world is concerned, you have died all over.   Go and be happy ! "

And Abou dismissed him, and resumed his experiments.

XI.

HOW TO WIN SUCCESS IN LITERATURE.

ABOU BEN ADHEM had a mortal dread of young literary persons. Whenever he saw a man of tender age, with long hair, a turn-over collar, and fine dreamy eyes, he was in the habit of calling loudly for his shot-gun. He disliked them more, if possible, than he did book-agents or life-insurance solicitors.

It was with great surprise, therefore, that one morning I saw a young man of this description enter his enclosure and approach the sage without the latter indulging in any ferocious demonstrations.

"Well?" said Abou.

"Great man, Light of the world I may say, — help me, aid me! I have a call, a mission. I have within me yearnings for the Good, the True, the Beautiful. The Grand inspires me; the Sublime exalts me. I would write for the weekly papers. How shall I achieve my purpose?"

"Young man," said Abou, "I was once like you. I wrote for the sake of Suffering Humanity. The check which I received for each article, though it shed a ray of light over the heart of my landlady, was not the impelling motive, it was merely an agreeable incident.

"A desire to benefit Suffering Humanity always guided my pen. It was a sweet thing, I found, to live solely for the good of others. That is what I did. It was my best hold. I wrote for the good of the human race. When I did not publish, I did what good I could by reading my work to a friend (a man of great bodily strength and wonderful powers of endurance), that at least one might be benefited. I took the manuscript of an article to him once, and, to my great grief, found him sick with a fever.

"'My dear sir,' said I, 'how much, for your sake, do I regret this unlucky illness! Were you well, I should read you this manuscript.'

"'Is it yours?' he asked, feebly.

"'It is.'

"'Were I well you would read it to me?'

"'Most certainly.'

"A smile illumined his wan, pale, fever-wasted face, as the light of the sun struggles through the rifts of a leaden cloud, and glorifies the brow of a gray rock. There was in that smile a wonderful commingling, as it were, of resignation, thankfulness, and joy.

"'Were I well, you would read me your manuscript, eh? How kindly Providence has arranged things! The bitter is not altogether bitter, nor is the good altogether good. Even typhoid fever has its compensations.'

"I am willing to waste some time on you, for I presume it is your intention to elevate the tone of American literature. It needs elevating, and I have been waiting in vain for some one to elevate it. What have we, in the way of magazines or papers, that are proper exponents of the best thought of the country? What kind of an idea would the *literati* of the Old World have of American literature, if they saw only the issues of the periodical press of the country? Echo answers. The "Atlantic Monthly" has, as a rule, some good things in each number, but is too light, too airy, too frisky. The "North American Review" suits, of course, a certain class of readers, but its levity is unendurable. It lacks that weight, that dignity, that a quarterly ought always to possess; and as for the other magazines — well, I will say nothing about them, but I have my opinion.

"Writers are needed who do things with a purpose. For instance, if you write tales, let them be always moral tales. Have your village maiden always in simple book-muslin, with a simple blue sash about her waist, tripping in a simple manner to the grove beyond the green, to meet John Perkins, the brawny bricklayer, her lover. Have her marry him, despite the warnings of her guardian, who has discovered that John Perkins plays seven-up at a quarter a corner, and five-cent poker, and other sinful games, and what is still more heinous, invariably loses. After the wedding, have John Perkins go on from seven-up to tobacco, from tobacco to rum; make him the frequent father of cherub children, who shall always be in rags; make him whip his wife regularly; and finally, when at the lowest round of the ladder, have him saved by an itinerant temperance lecturer, to the great delight of his wife, who shall suddenly grow young again, and shall adopt book-muslin and blue sashes, and lean trustingly on his arm, as she did in the days before the fall, and have John go into the temperance missionary business himself, and so forth.

"This style of writing is done easily when you are once ready for it, but it requires a deal of preparation. A man of ordinary intellect would require a month of the wildest and most debasing dissipation to reduce his mind to the level for it. But in the interest of moral writing, you should be willing to do even this.

"If you write stories of real life, indulge in no vagaries. In your stories the young man must always marry the girl, and the would-be seducer must always commit suicide when he fails in his hellish designs, leaving his ill-gotten gains to the young man who was his nephew, though no one knew it or suspected it till he came to the point of expiring. Right there make an impressive moral picture. The young man must refuse to take the blood-stained gold, and must say, "Never mind it, Sophia; we are poor, but I would beg on the streets rather than live in luxury upon money every piece of which is dark with the bel-lud of innocence, and rusted with the tears of the helpless. We are poor, Sophia: let us be virtuous." In real life, he probably would n't say anything of the kind.   He would have taken the shekels if each individual shekel had been voted its possessor as back-pay.   He would have set up a carriage, Sophia would have indulged in cargoes of fine dresses, and they would have made it lively in their neighborhood.   But in your stories, always have the hero say, "We are poor, but let us be virtuous."   The poor generally are virtuous — is it because they have n't the ducats to be wicked with? It is a conundrum of the most exhaustive nature.

"And in your stories Virtue must always triumph over Vice.   Adhere steadily to Virtue.   I have a respect for Virtue.   Familiarity with her has not yet bred contempt.   I believe in giving Virtue fair play; and as in actual life, Vice, as a rule, comes out winner by a great many lengths, I insist that in romance Virtue shall have a show.   If she does n't get it there, where will she?

"Avoid, carefully, all naturalness in writing.   We can get naturalness anywhere — we have a surfeit of it.   Mud is natural: mix water and dirt, and you have it.   But is it attractive?   The people very properly want something beside nature if they are expected to pay for it, for nature they can get for nothing.   Who cares for blue water?   No one.   Let the bay turn to a bright red, and everybody would rush to see it.   We gaze at the sun only when it is eclipsed. How many people would go a step out of their way to see two perfectly formed, handsome men?   To put this so that it will be perfectly plain to the dullest, how many citizens of New York would go to see Roscoe Conkling and myself? None. But how many hundreds of thousands of people paid half-dollars to see that pigmy, Tom Thumb, and those solemn, spirit-depressing curiosities, the Siamese Twins? Had the tie been severed that bound those willing hearts, not a man or woman in Christendom would have gone after them, unless to have seen what was left of the tie.

" The attractiveness of Dickens' sweet little female children consists entirely in the startling fact that children of that style are not lying around loose. They are seen only in his pages and in Sunday-school papers, where the precocious prigs propound heavy questions in theology to their gratified parents, and save up their pennies for the heathen. If you write for children, draw all your portraits from this class.

" You may, possibly, try a tale of the Revolution. If so, you may depend upon it that the young plough-man who left his horses in the field to join the patri-ots will always taunt his captors with being red-coated tools of British tyranny ; that he will always refuse a Brigadier-General's commission in the Brit-ish army, preferring starvation as a private in the service of his bleeding country. In describing bat-tles, you must always have the proud Britons two to our one, and you must always defeat the proud Brit-ons, though the painful impression is on my mind that history shows that whenever the Continentals and British came together in a hostile way, your gal-lant forefathers were, as a rule, most satisfactorily whaled.

"You may, also, try your versatile hand on an Indian romance. If so, the elegant triflers, fresh from Broadway, must always excel the noble red man of the forest in rifle-shooting and woodcraft generally, and must always succeed in circumventing and destroying the cunning savage on his own ground, and with his own weapons.

"You must not startle anybody by going outside of what is regular.

"But romance may not be your best hold. You may prefer to cheer a despondent public with cheerful essays of a light and playful character, on such familiar subjects as 'The Origin of the Human Race,' 'The Connection of Animal with Vegetable Life,' or something of that sort, straying from the path occasionally to pluck a few flowers from the tariff statistics or the currency question. If so, follow the same rule as in romance. Avoid a fact as you would the small-pox or a reformer. Let your theories contain just the one point that will please the most people, and generalize the words of six syllables in sentences so long that the strongest memory will forget the beginning before it comes to the ending. The reader will never understand you, and will deem you truly wise. We always look up to that which we cannot understand. In Persia, my young friend, were once a set of *illuminati*, very like those you have in your country, who spake only in six-syllabled words. I cursed myself for an idiot one day because I could not comprehend a speech that one of them made. After hammering on it for two weeks, I thought I smelt something. I took my dictionary and tackled the great words ; I translated it, in short, into the Persian of every-day use, and found what? It was an article of my own that I had written for the 'Ispahan Morning Herald,' nothing more or less. The metaphysical fraud had merely clothed it in words of six syllables.

"Remember this : There is nothing like words of six syllables to hide commonplaces and platitudes.

"Follow these directions, my infant, and in time you may get to the height of getting four dollars a column for your work in the weekly papers, which is fame.

"Away, for I have done. Peace be with thee ! "

XII.

THE WISE OLD RAT.

ABOU BEN ADHEM was asked by a young man from Boston this question: "Is it possible for man, limited as are his powers, surrounded as he is by circumstances, driven hither and yon as he is by influences outside himself, to lay out a course in life and follow it; that is to say, can man, imperfect as he is, repressed by the inevitable, circumscribed by the unscalable, and assailed by the irresistible, go forward and rise into a higher, purer, and better life in a straight line, or must he deviate at points in his progress to evade obstacles, and —"

"State that again, young man, for I fain would comprehend you," said Abou.

"What I want to know is this: Can man, limited as he is —"

"Now I comprehend what you want to know," said Abou, promptly. "Why did n't you state it that way before? Clearness in statement is necessary. I will answer your question by a parable written by Cheesit, a sage of Brownith, who was beheaded for embezzlement some two hundred years

ago. The legend (it is a poem in the original) runs
thus : —

"Once upon a time, a wise old rat, whose gray
hairs attested his age, left his peaceful home in search
of food for his numerous progeny. It was a beautiful evening. The sun was descending o'er the
western hills, investing their summits with a coronal
of gold, and transforming the banks of clouds into
seas of liquid light. The birds sang their vesper
hymns, the dormouse chirped its faint pee-wee, taking care to get into its hole as rapidly as convenient,
for the dormouse knew that he was a toothsome
morsel, and that the rat is constitutionally hungry.
The young chickens chirped cheerily, but they too
absented themselves with alacrity at his approach,
for they knew that the softness of the evening, and
the general harmony, as it were, of things in general,
would not prevent that rat from taking them in.
They would have said as much could they have
spoken. Alas! that there is no such thing as perfect peace. The chicken eats the worm, the rat eats
the chicken, the terrier eats the rat. Is this the
warring of forces, or is it stomach? Is it the eternal order of things, or is it appetite? It is a conundrum, — I give it up. But it is sad.

"He tripped along gayly, for the splendor of the
evening filled his soul. He murmured somewhat
at the lack of confidence in the fat dormouse and
the juicy chicken, but not much. He was musing
over the events of a long life; of the granaries
he had gnawed into; of the dogs he had avoided;

and was repeating to himself that grand poem of Zoo-
Zoo's, —

'Life is real, life is earnest,' —

When the familiar sound 'Hi!' startled him from his
pleasant revery.

"One glance, and he took in the situation. He
was in a garden which afforded no opportunity for
concealment, and within ten feet of him stood a small
but intensely wicked boy, who had a brick poised in
his hand, and was about hurling it full at him.

"Whiz! came the deadly missile. An adroit
spring backward saved him, when the boy gave
chase. The rat saw an old house near, and towards
that he ran, hoping to find in its purlieus friendly
shelter. Alas! for the hunted fugitive. He made
one mighty leap, and experienced a sense of falling.
He found himself in the bottom of a dry cistern,
seventeen feet deep, whose smooth walls it was impossible to scale. The boy saw the trap the rat had
fallen into, and was quickly on the spot. Another
brick was convenient, and that was immediately
hurled. Fortunately the aim of the boy was not
perfect. Ill had it fared with that rat if this had been
ten years later in life, when that boy, grown to be a
man, had run with a fire-company in New York, and
had learned to hurl the brick with unerring aim!

"A shingle lay near, and that he threw with no
better success than before, but as he searched for
another missile, he bethought himself.

"'He can't get out,' pondered this cruel boy. 'I

will let him stay, and in the morning I will bring Nip, my terrier, and chuck him in the cistern with the rat, and won't he make that rat sick, though?'

"By making 'that rat sick, though,' this vigorous but unrefined youth meant to say that the terrier dog would rend the rodent. He had never attended school, and had not learned to express himself properly.

"He turned away with a sardonic smile o'erspreading his otherwise intelligent countenance.

"The wails of the entrapped one soon brought to the spot his wife and her multitude of children, who, falling on their hind-quarters around the edge of the cistern, wrung their paws in agony and cried, —

"'Bald-head, come up!'

"'Verily would I,' returned he, 'but how? No, my children, it's up with me. My time is almost gone. With daylight comes the boy, with the boy the dog, and I shall pass in my chips. I'm a goner, my time is short. Bless you, wife of my bosom! Bless you, products of our chaste love! I had hoped to live, my children, long enough to have taught you the neatest way of gnawing through a cupboard, the most expeditious way of spoiling a carpet, — my way, by which it can never be repaired. I had hoped I might teach you how to dodge a cat, how to avoid a terrier, how to suck eggs, and all the learning that experience has brought me. But hope fails me; it is all of no avail. Fate is too many for me; I succumb. But I will die like a rat — with dignity. That terrier will bear with him marks of my claws.

To superior strength will I yield, to nothing else. My body may be shaken, but my undaunted soul, never! I would I had a Roman toga, that I might pull it over my head when I die, as Cæsar did. But one can't have effective accessories in a cistern. It is n't a good place for a heroic death.'

"At this minute a heavy rain commenced.

"'Now,' said he, 'I am surely destroyed. The cistern will fill with water, and I shall drown. Oh, wretched fate! what a ghastly corpse I shall make. For what is more horrid than a drowned rat!'

"The rain increased in severity, and soon the bottom of the cistern was covered. In his despair the rat noticed that the shingle, which the boy had hurled at him, floated, and to prolong his life he sprang upon it, much to the disappointment of his youngest, who had a natural curiosity to see how their progenitor would look floundering in the water. Perched thus, he began to disclose to his wife the location of a cheese he had lately discovered.

"'My dear wife,' he was saying, 'it wrings my heart to leave you, but I must. Why, oh! why must we be separated just as life was becoming worth having? Why must I be taken just as I had learned to love you, and you had learned to love me? Oh, the agony of death, now that I see you! But take courage, dearest. There is another world, and to that you will come, and paw in paw we will go through an eternity in a land that has no wicked boys or terriers. But I will make your stay as comfortable as possible. Before I die, dearest, let me say that the

cheese is in the pantry at Zaba's.   Go for it.   You
will go through the sewer — '

"At this moment he observed that the shingle bore
him with perfect ease, and he immediately ceased to
talk.

"'Go on! go on!' said his wife, horrified at the
possibility of a secret so valuable dying with him,
'Go on, go on!'

"'Shut up, you old fool you!' said he, resuming
his regular style with great promptness. 'If this
rain holds on long enough, I am as good as a dozen
dead rats.'

"And sure enough, he did not perish.   On that
shingle he held; the rain continued until the cistern
was quite full, and he paddled to the edge with his
front paws, steering with his tail, and gayly sprang
on terra firma (which is the Latin for dry land), and
was safe.

"He had made his escape.   The boy came next
morning with his terrier, but the rat was not there to
rend.   The boy was disappointed, and so likewise
was the terrier, but what was evil for them was good
for the rat.

"That evening the wise old rat sat in his humble
domicile, contented and happy.   He gathered his
children about him, and deduced from his late adven-
ture the usual moral lesson.   He never forgot the
moral.

"'Observe, my children,' said he, 'that blessings
come to us very frequently in disguise.   We murmur
at terriers which rend us with neatness and dispatch,

and with a celerity which is a perpetual surprise to me. But mark! had not this wicked boy had a terrier he would have dispatched me with bricks. He would have heaved them, and heaved them, till it was dark, and then he would have gone and got a lantern, by the light of which he would have continued to heave. Thus are the evil desires of the wicked made to work good for the saints. I am a saint.

"'How I dreaded those bricks! Yet but for a brick to stand on, the rain would have drowned me in the first five minutes.

"'That shingle was another terror. Yet, but for that shingle, your progenitor would have been that most disgusting of all things — a drowned rat.

"'The rain was to have been my destruction — that was to have overwhelmed me. Blessed was that rain! Without that rain of what good would have been that brick and shingle? That rain lifted me out of the pit into which I had fallen; the flood which was to have drowned me bore me on its bosom to safety.

"'In conclusion, my children: Providence always furnishes opportunities to every one. The truly great is he who makes good use of opportunities, he who sees what is worth his while to grab, and has the nerve to do it.

"'Never despair is an exceedingly good motto. Keep your eyes peeled, your ears open, and your claws sharp, and there is no trouble about your going through life with a wet sheet and a flowing sail. My late experience, my dears, accounts for my nautical mode of expression. Remember there is no evil but is mixed with good; that the wise turn evil to good, while the foolish sink under it. Bless you, my children, I will seek my couch."

"My young friend," said Abou, "this is the legend. Does it answer your question, or are you not sufficiently intellectual to comprehend parables? I repeat, are you answered?"

The young man from Boston looked at Abou and said, —

"What I want to know is this: Is man partially developed, imper —"

"You told me all that once before, and my legend answered it. Go to, young man! Do you laugh at me? Am I a man? Bismallah! —"

And Abou's face assumed such an expression of ferocity that the mild young man from Boston abruptly fled his presence.

As he left him, a soft smile broke over Abou's countenance, and the expression of wrath was gone.

"By hokey! — that is to say, Be chesm! — my answer was as intelligible as his question. May Allah keep me from young men of 'culcha'!"

And Abou went into his laboratory.

XIII.

WEALTH.

ABOU BEN ADHEM sat in front of his tent one beautiful morning in August, looking out calmly on the scene that lay before him. On the one side were the long ranges of hills ; before him the beautiful stream meandered cosily through the rich bottom, its sides dotted with sleek cattle, which, intent upon the rich grass, fed quietly, unmindful of the mosquitoes that were buzzing about them. Abou's soul was filled with the beauty of the scene.

" Why," said he, "should we not take a lesson from the cows ? Why should we not enjoy the great good we have, and not notice the small troubles that beset us ? Why should we not, with the wealth of delights we possess, permit ourselves to be absorbed in enjoyment, and despise the trifling troubles of life ? I loathe the man who permits little things to make him lose his temper, and — May Allah curse that evil-minded and altogether aggravating fly ! What were such pests permitted for ? "

And Abou, vigorously slapping his cheek in endeavors to kill the fly, poured forth a flood of the

choicest Persian profanity.   Alas! like all philos-
ophers, Abou could not follow his own philosophy.
The contemplation of nature upset by a fly!

Scarcely had he smitten his head thrice, in vain
attempts to kill the fly, when a young man appeared.

" Well! " was Abou's greeting.

" Do I stand in the presence of Abou ben Adhem? "

" You have that felicity!   What will you with
him? "

" Mighty Abou — "

" Don't say *mighty* Abou.   Be chesm, it has become monotonous.   Change it, or cheese it! "

(Abou frequently dropped into the Oriental style.)

" Great Abou (if that suits you better), I am an
humble suppliant."

" Get at it now, get at it!   Of course you are an
humble suppliant.   You did n't come here to do *me*
good.   No, indeed, no one ever does.   But to business.   What is your particular form of idiocy? "

" Great Abou, I would be rich.   I would have
gold, or National Bank notes (I am not particular),
and would enjoy all that money can buy.   I would —"

" Young man," said Abou, " that is a very common
form of insanity, and very hard to cure.   Every man
who is unable to lift himself up from the common
level by any other means tries to do it by accumulating money; every man who lusts after the pleasures of life yearns for money to buy them.   Then
there is the grovelling man, who wants money for the
sake of money; and the more dangerous man, who

desires it for the power it wields. I will give you
five minutes of wisdom. When you hear me say 'I
have done,' what you want to do is to get out of this
as rapidly as possible."

And Abou significantly cocked a double-barrelled
shot-gun, and set it down blandly within easy reach,
and drove on the cart of his discourse.

"To accumulate money, my young friend, is the
easiest thing in the world. All you have to do is to
make a dollar a day, and spend only seventy-five
cents. Any grovelling worm in worldly dust, any
puller and hauler of the worldly muck-rake who
knows enough to realize that one hundred cents make
a dollar, and who, at the same time, is too infernally
mean to spend any part of it, may become as rich as
Crœsus, if he don't starve to death too soon. To
amass shekels, all that is necessary is to live like a
beggar, and write the word 'grub' in your hat, if
indeed you allow yourself the luxury of a hat. You
must, however, go through the process of eliminating
from your nature everything in the shape of love,
charity, mercy, tenderness, liberality, warmth, geni-
ality, taste, and all desire for enjoyment of any kind.
I have known men who had as much money as they
could use, who would deliberately live away from
their families ten months in the year, to make more;
and this, too, when all the comfort they ever had
was with their families. Money must fill the entire
man, and the accumulation thereof be the sole pleasure and passion. Accomplish this, and you will find
your money will grow as fast as you desire it.

"But *you* will decrease.   The love of money is a
tape-worm, — it feeds on the body that carries it.
Your soul will shrink, and shrivel, and fade, till you
will have none of it whatever.   You have seen a
tumble-bug in your native New Jersey, rolling a ball
of dirt.   It rolls and rolls till the ball is bigger than
the bug, and it can't roll any farther, when it lies
down and dies by the side of its accumulation.   Precisely so, my rash friend, you will roll up money
till it gets too large to manage, and you will lie
down and die by the side of it.

"There are, of course, other ways of accumulating.
You might take a revolver and go on the highway;
there is forgery, pocket-picking, getting into Congress and voting yourself back-pay, and other modes;
but being of a good family, and expecting to have
children of your own, of course you would n't think
of doing anything of the kind.

"We now come to the second part of this chunk
of wisdom.   What are you going to do with your
wealth when you have it?   Enjoy yourself, eh?
Yes, they all say so.   But when your strength is all
gone, what have you got to enjoy yourself with?
Your table?   What good is a French cook when
your stomach, used up by the labor of years, won't
allow you to eat?   Society?   What good is society
to a man who has been educating himself for forty
years in nothing but stocks and merchandise?
Travel?   You would n't endure it a month, because
what you saw you would n't comprehend.   Probably
the most touching sight in Nature is a venerable,

gray-haired pork-packer at an opera, or in front of a picture. You see, the effort necessary to make money exhausts all the faculties which you expect money to cater for.

"It so happens, or rather it is wisely ordered, that trouble is the twin-brother of every one of the pleasures that money buys. Champagne tickles the palate and looks well in a glass, but gout hides in every bubble. The smiling face of the scarlet woman has an angel's look, but — well, get one tacked to you and see what will happen! The dinner of eleven courses makes a pleasant show and a goodly; but behind the waiter stalks dyspepsia, grim and terrible. Your money brings it all; you can't take half and leave half; it goes all in one lot.

"Then what is it worth, anyhow? The inexpensive but thirst-quenching beer curls me as beautifully o'er the beaker's brim as the costly champagne, and is, after all, as good, if you only think so. The mysterious hash, flavored with the long-reaching onion, is as appetizing as the *pâte de foie gras*, — the one costing a shilling and the other ten dollars. The kabob of veal, which in Ispahan can be had for a kopack, is as toothsome as the pilau of lamb for which the true believer shells out a dirhem. One thing, my infant, is as good as another thing, and, doubtless, better. Were the waters of the rivulet champagne, and were water worth four dollars and a half per bottle, with a fee to the waiter, the men of wealth would all be smacking their lips over water. Whiskey rasps our interiors as effectually as brandy;

the one is within the reach of the humblest purse,
the other is so many ducats per gallon. A carriage
is a good enough thing in its way, but heavens!
think of being a slave to a coachman! And having
the carriage, you feel that you must ride in it whether
or no. Imagine a condition of things that compels
you to ride whether or no! What a weight a carriage must be on one's mind! And then, again,
think of the terror that an average servant in a black
coat and white neck-tie must inspire!

"My dear sir, a state approximating to vagabond-
age is the state in which the most happiness is found.
Happiness means simply freedom from all care, save
that which delights you. I fain would be an Italian
prince, exiled from my native soil, gaining a subsist-
ence by grinding a hand-organ. Or I would be an
Ethiopian, earning an honest though precarious living by doing odd jobs about houses and picking up
such trifles as can be conveniently reached. These
men have no troubles. The sixpence of the morning
gives them a dinner, the five-cent piece of the after-
noon a supper, and a dry-goods box a bed. I never
heard of an organ-grinder who owned a big railroad
to worry over, or a boot-black who bought care in
the form of a steamship line. But they live, move,
and have being, and what more does Vanderbilt?

"Go to, young man, go to! Strive to be like me.
You probably never will reach the height of philosophical virtue on which I repose, but you may
come something near it. Despise money; do not
waste a life in pursuit of it. Do as I do, — learn

to live without it, to care nothing for it, and be happy."

And Abou, having finished his homily, sold a Durham heifer to the young man at a bargain, and a hundred shares in a Texas railway. And chuckling at the ease with which he had taken him in for a thousand dollars, he turned to his labor.

XIV.

THE PHILOSOPHY OF KOAB.

ABOU BEN ADHEM was approached one day by a young man who asked him as to the best method of using up an inheritance he had just fallen into. Abou looked at the young man; he diagnosed the case, as it were, and went for him thus : —

"Young man, I will tell you a story of Persian life. Listen.

"Koab, the son of Beslud, the leather merchant, was a young man of twenty when his paternal progenitor was promoted to be an angel and assumed wings. Koab did not weep at his father's demise, for the old gentleman had accumulated his lucre with great care and by great labor, and, consequently, was very, very close with it. He had been a singular old man. He never knew the taste of champagne, and always smoked a pipe, — excellent preparation for death, methinks. With such tastes, what was there for him to live for? What was there in death for him to fear?

"But he left young Koab a fortune of an even

hundred thousand dirhems, which the young man lost
no time in transferring to his own keeping.

"Immediately Koab's relatives gathered about him
to advise him as to what to do with it.

"One said, 'Go into the grocery business and become a merchant prince.' Another strongly insisted
that his best hold was to go into railroads with his
capital, and be a Van-der-Built. Another advised,
with tears in his eyes, that he go into dry goods and
be a Stoo-art or a Klaa-flynn. Another was divided
in opinion as to whether he ought to start a daily
paper or run a theatre; but Koab dismissed him
with a frown. 'He hates me, and would ruin me
quickly,' quoth the sagacious young man.

"'I shall do nothing of the sort,' said he. 'I shall
adopt none of your suggestions.'

"'You will be ruined if you do not!' shouted they
all in a chorus.

"'As not one of you has succeeded in making a
fortune,' retorted Koab, 'it strikes me that you are
fearfully competent to advise me. But I have marked
out my path in life.'

"'What is it?'

"'I shall, firstly, get rid of all my poor relations.

"The relatives all discharged themselves of groans.

"'Then I shall invest what the old m— that is, my
poor father, left me, in safe securities bearing ten per
cent.'

"'Good! that will give you ten thousand dirhems
per year.'

"'True, but I shall not live on ten thousand per

year. I shall live on about twenty thousand a year. I shall have horses, an interest in a yacht, shall join all the clubs, shall never drink water when wine is attainable; in short, I shall go for pleasure in every possible way that pleasure is to be had.'

" 'But you will run through your fortune while you are still young.'

" 'That is the time to run it through, while I am young enough to enjoy it. What, O idiots! is the good of a fine dinner to a man whose stomach is worn out and who is too much used up to eat it? Wherefore wine to him whose stomach can't abide wine? Wherefore anything to a man who can't take anything? I would prefer it, had I income enough, to live just as I desire without infringing upon my capital; but as I cannot, I propose to live my life anyhow. Fate has been cruel to me in not giving me two hundred thousand dirhems. I shall never feel pleasant towards my deceased father that he did not labor harder and live more savingly. He has used me badly. But I am a philosopher. Koab proposes now to drain the cup of pleasure to its dregs.'

" Koab went in, in the language of the prize ring, in a very spirited style. He kept a fast horse, he drank wine, he gambled a little; and if his feminine friends had been virtuous in proportion to the amount of money he spent on them, Cæsar's wife would have been a drab in comparison with them. But they were not. On the contrary, quite the reverse.

" He had a severe fit of sickness, which nursed his

estate a little ; but he managed by hard work to get through with the most of it in about ten years.

" 'Your money must be nearly all gone,' said his friends to him one day.

" 'I have about a thousand dirhems left,' said he.

" 'Horrible !' said they.

" 'Beautiful !' said he. 'My stomach is also almost gone. How lovely it is to have your money hold out as long as your stomach ! Had one given out before the other, — I shudder at the thought. To have an appetite and no money, or to have no appetite and cords of money, — I know not which is the worst. But with me it is splendid. Things run in grooves, as it were. A few more dinners, a few more nights, and my stomach will be gone, and my money with it. But I *have* had a good time of it.'

" 'What will you do then ?'

" 'Impious wretch, do you read Holy Writings? " Sufficient for the day is the evil thereof." In my case, I can testify to the truth of that passage every day. Then again, " Take no thought of the morrow." ' '

" As he anticipated, in a few weeks Koab had not a dirhem, not a kopeck left. He lived a few days on credit, and then spent several days considering whether suicide by poison or drowning was the more pleasant. After giving the subject mature consideration, he concluded that he would not die at all, and accepted a situation as a porter in a wholesale grocery store, whose proprietor had known his father.

" He was rolling barrels one day, when his friends came in.

"'Ha!' said they. 'You see, now, we were right: you are brought down to manual labor at thirty.'

"'Precisely what my physician would have prescribed for a wasted constitution like mine,' said he, cheerfully. 'I am gaining flesh under it.'

"They came in again, and saw him eating brown bread.

"'Ha!' they remarked. 'You are brought down to plain food. We told you so.'

"'My friends,' said he, impressively, 'were I the possessor of millions, I should, after ten years of dissipation, be compelled to eat plain food or die. O ye imbeciles! can't you see that this is natural? What difference does it make whether I eat brown bread by the advice of a physician, or eat it because I can't get any other? What difference does it make whether I exercise my overtaxed body in a gymnasium, where I pay for the privilege, or exercise it by rolling barrels, for which I get paid? "Exercise and plain food," said my doctor long ago, "is what you must have." I am getting both, ye sodden-brained Job's comforters.'

"And Koab worked on, and got his health, and finally got into business, and made money, and had another fortune to spend; and he spent it.

"This, my young friend, is all of the story of Koab, the Persian, that I shall tell you. There is a moral to it which probably you don't see. But I have a comfortable way of fixing people who do not see the moral to the things I say. I simply say it is because they lack the necessary intellect.

"Far be it from me to advise young men to squander their fortunes in riotous living, as did Koab. Koab's idea was not wholly correct. He erred.

"But he erred no more than do those who go to the other extreme; in fact, he erred less.

"The people who grub through their entire youth, enjoying nothing, with the idea that they will live to enjoy at some remote period, err a great deal more, for the reason that they never enjoy at all. Grubbing unfits them for enjoying, and therefore their labor is to no purpose. Kunla, the Persian poet, who wrote 'Go it while you're young,' was not wholly wrong; for youth has the faculty to enjoy and the power to enjoy. The blood courses freely; there is strength, elasticity, and joyousness. But alas! there comes a time when we cannot enjoy if we would. The man of sixty, *sans* teeth, *sans* gastric juice, *sans* stomach, thin-blooded, cold, and cynical, can enjoy but little at best; and if he has grubbed in his youth, ten to one but he has acquired a habit of grubbing which lasts him through his old age, and his life may be said to be as much of a failure as the other.

"If Koab had been a moral person, and had enjoyed himself in a rational way, within his income, and had done some business for the sake of others, I should mark on his tombstone 'Approved.' He should have had his yacht; he should have eaten good dinners; he should have had the fleet horses of Arabia; and he should have had pictures and all else that pleases the senses. But he should have avoided

excesses and immoralities ; he should have used some
of his money in relieving the necessities of the unfortunate children of the Prophet ; in short, he should
have paid the debt which we all owe to humanity.

"But as between Koab and the man who uses his
inheritance only to double it, who lives a life only to
gather dross without putting it to any use whatever,
I give my voice to Koab as the most sensible.

" My son, some day when I have time I will write
you a history of *my* life, which you shall read, and
which will be a lamp to your feet, and a sure guide.

"But leave me now, for I fain would rest.
Away ! "

And Abou went in to count over the profits of a
speculation he had been in; and he wrought at it
late in the night.

" Why do you so labor for lucre ? " said I to him.
" Do you follow the lesson you gave the young man,
O Sage ? "

" What says Hafiz ? " was his reply : " Chin-music
is cheaper even than that of the hand-organ.' Doth
advice cost ? Go to ! "

XV.

THE DANGER THAT LIES IN THE NAMING OF CHILDREN AFTER GREAT MEN.

ABOU BEN ADHEM was called upon one day by a person who desired to apply the suction-pump to him. The man — for it was a male person — had with him a bright-faced, intelligent boy of perhaps six summers, who was restless and impatient, as such boys are likely to be. The lad broke loose from his father, and ran to chase a butterfly that was lazily disporting itself in the warm air, when the father, with tender solicitude, said to him, —

"Schuyler Colfax, remain with your parent! You might slip up and soil your pants, my child."

As the father spoke these words, an expression of pain flitted over the countenance of the sage.

"Your name is Thompson?"

"It is."

"And your che-ild's name is Schuyler Colfax Thompson?"

"It is."

"Alas! poor child."

"Why do you sigh and say 'Alas! poor child'?"

"Because Schuyler Colfax is not yet dead, and a grateful country has not, as yet, bedewed his untimely grave with tears. That's why I sigh for that sweet child. Listen.

"I was once a sweet child myself, — the pride of a loving father and of a darling mother. When I was born Agha Ilderim was the vast artillery of the province. He was a member of the Council, he was the great orator, and, in short, the coming man. My father was a warm supporter of the great Agha Ilderim: he was on his committees at elections, and he attended all his meetings, and rallied his voters to the polls, and brought in the aged and infirm voters, and was as enthusiastic a supporter of the great man as he could wished to have had. And it was purely disinterested too. True, the fact that my father had been appointed, by Agha, inspector of rat-terriers for that district, was urged by his enemies as a reason for his zeal; but it was a slander.

"When I was born Agha Ilderim was at the zenith of his power, and my father, the moment the sex of the child was ascertained, threw up his turban and named it Agha Ilderim, and Agha gave me a silver cup and patted me on the head, and predicted a glorious future for me.

"But alas! when I was five years old there came a trouble upon Agha Ilderim. There was a road that was being built by the government and there was a huge swindle in it. The Shah investigated it, and lo! it was discovered that Agha had had his arms in it elbow-deep, and once opened, it was discovered that this patriot had been speculating and stealing in every possible way, for years. And he was disgraced of course, and defeated for the Council, and became of nought among men, and his name became a hissing and by-word, and in his stead rose Nadir el Abin, who took Agha's place and became the great man of the province.

" My father became a great admirer of Nadir, and, as he was continued in his office, did for Nadir what he had done for Agha. Filled with indignation at the dishonesty of Agha, he melted the silver cup he had given me, and sold it, and spent the proceeds in strong waters, and immediately changed my name to Nadir el Abin, and was happy.

" But lo! in about four years the Governor of the province desired to get through the Council a measure which the people did not approve of, because it took away their liberties. The members of the Council were implored to stand firm against the usurpation, and Nadir was looked upon as one of the most trustworthy; but, to the indignation of the people, he voted with the Governor, and carried the measure, and when they hooted at him he put his finger to his nose, for the Governor made him Collector of Revenue for life.

Then was my father's rage kindled against Nadir, and he came home and said to my mother, —

" ' Lo! Nadir's name is a stench in the nostrils of the people. Be chesm, it will never do for our child to bear the name of Nadir.'

"And as Akbar, the scribe, vaulted into Nadir's

place in the affections of the people, my name was forthwith changed to Akbar.

" Akbar ran well for a season, but he went under. A patent for tipping chibouques was before the Council for extension, and the people murmured at it, for it offended them. The owners of the patent, however, cared nothing for that. They appeared to the members of the Council with arguments, in bags, and Akbar was possessed of many bags immediately after he had voted to extend the patent, and the people hooted him and threw mud at him in the market-place.

" As a matter of course it would not do for me to continue to bear the name of Akbar, and it was changed to that of Hafiz, and when he went under, to Katah, which I kept till Katah succumbed because he voted himself back-pay and was concerned in a ring for building a road.

" Then my father and mother held a council over me one morning.

" ' I have tried," said my paternal parent, " to give our child an honorable name.'

" ' Verily,' returned my mother.

" ' But whenever I gave him the name of a great man, that man suddenly deceased, that is, politically.'

" ' He did,' said my mother ; ' it is fate.'

" ' What shall we do?' asked my father. ' The child must have a name, and it seems to be risky to give him the name of any one living. Advise me, O my wife ! '

" ' Let the great men go, for lo ! such is the construction of the human mind, that greatness is as

uncertain as railroad stocks.   Let us call him
Abou.'

"And they did it.   Abou, my friend, is a name
which, in Persia, is as common as John is in New
Jersey.

" And now comes the point.   Change that boy's
name from Schuyler Colfax to plain James, John, or
Thomas.   Never name a child after any living greatness.   If you must name him after a great man, take
a dead one, and select a very dead one.   Go to your
books and roust out a deceased statesman.   Avoid
your recent ones.   Go back and find one who has
been dead so long that all his vices and peccadilloes
have been obliterated by the hand of time, and only
his virtues remembered.   I would advise you not to
fasten on any one who has flourished since the Roman Empire.   It will not answer to take a living man,
for his balance-sheet is not made up till he has gone
hence.   A gone-hencer is safe, and no one else is.
Imagine the feelings of that parent who, just after
the battle of Saratoga, in your Revolution, named
his innocent child Benedict Arnold !   The hero of
Saratoga may always become the traitor of West
Point.   To bring it down to a later date, what is to
become of the thousands of children who, between
the years 1860 and 1867, were named A. Johnson?

" My friend, for names go among the dead men.
Their lives are closed and their balances are struck.
A man dead, with worms at him, and under several
tons of marble monument, cannot possibly get up
and blast a fair reputation.   So long as a man lives

he is in danger.   Folly, and greed, and ambition surround every man who lives.   I have to fight them off myself.

"Change the name of your child to Thomas at once.   And go, for I am weary."

XVI.

OLD TIMES AND NEW.

THE Persian, Abou ben Adhem, was in a deep study one morning, when a person — a male person — from the village in the neighborhood came to him for the purpose of conversation.

"What wouldst thou?" was Abou's remark.

"I would learn something!" was the reply.

"That is to say, you would drop the bucket of your ignorance into the well of my wisdom. Well, be chesm, drop away! what wouldst thou now?"

"Great Abou, is there any way by which we degenerate sons of noble sires can get back to the good old habits, manners, and customs of our forefathers? Can we restore the simple habits of the olden time, — the good old time?"

"What?"

"Can we not go back a few hundred years, and — "

"Ass!" was Abou's reply. "Oh, what a fate is mine! Such men as you come to me, and, as there is a punishment for killing, I am compelled to convert. Well, I submit.

"You sigh for the good old times, do you? Do

you know what those good old times were? Of
course you do not. Such men as you never do!
You have an idea in your wooden heads that men
were simple, honest beings, who went about in doublets, knee-breeches, and hose, with silver buckles on
their shoes; and that women were ditto,—all but the
breeches and doublets. You have got the notion
that as the world grows older wickedness increases,
and that all humanity is tending to a ghastly hell.
But I, who lived during those times, know better.

"O imbecile! O ignoramus! O unphilosoph-
ical reader of bad poetry! Don't you know that
human nature was precisely the same five hundred
years ago that it is now; that humanity perpetually
yearns for something better and higher and nobler,
and that precisely as knowledge increases so does
goodness? You want to go back to the good old
times, do you? What good old times? To the
good old times of Moses and Joshua, who had a habit
when they made war of slaughtering all the men,
women, and children that fell into their hands? No,
they reserved the women; but it was no compliment
to the morals of those people that they omitted that
much of bloodshed. Do you want to go back to the
good old times of the old French kings, — say Francis
and the earlier Louises, — when the people were
slaves, permitted black bread only, and not half
enough of that, and the nobles were tyrants, wield-
ing supreme power, and robed in velvets and silks?
Have you a fancy for the good old times in Germany,
when the barons, when they came in from hunting,

had a cheerful habit of having a peasant killed and
his bowels taken out that they might warm their feet
in the cavity?   Or do you prefer the good old times
in England, when king and court were so shamelessly
dissolute that no pretence of virtue was made, when
chastity was a scoff and concealment of sin a joke,
when London was ruled by common stabbers, when
might was right, and safety was only found in cunning or strength? How would you like to trade
your steamships for the old high-pooped sail-vessels,
the railroad for the cumbrous wagon, the macadamized
road for the mud, the cooking-range for the barbarous
fire, our cuisine for their fearful cookery, Croton
water for miserable wells, gas for torches of light-
wood, safety for danger, comfort for non-comfort, —
civilization for barbarism, in short?

"There was n't any such thing as humanity in those
days, either in theory or practice. If a man got
tired of his wife, he simply dissolved the matrimonial
tie by cutting her throat; if a woman got tired of her
husband, she hinted to her paramour the fact that Sir
Henry was a tiresome old muff, and immediately Sir
Henry had a rapier run through him.

"How vast the improvement of these later days!
Now the party disgusted simply goes to Indiana or
Chicago, and, in a perfectly legal manner, the judge
dissolves the connection, and the party returns and
marries the new object of his or her choice, and
everything is as serene as the face of a mill-pond.

"In the good old times of which you are so enam-
oured, if a man got embarrassed pecuniarily, he

142 *MORALS OF ABOU BEN ADHEM.*

mounted his horse and loaded his pistol, — they
did n't have beautiful revolvers then, — and putting
an ugly black mask over his face rode out on the
highway, and stopped the lumbering old coach, and
took purses at the muzzle of the pistol.

"Now how does such an individual do? Why, he
gets a contract from the Government, he starts a life
insurance company, or, if he is a great genius, a
genuine descendant of Dick Turpin or Jack Sheppard,
he gets into Congress, and votes as his conscience and
interest dictates, or he gets hold of the Erie Railroad,
or — but why enumerate? You see the difference,
and how much to-day is better than the days three
hundred years ago.

"To bring it down a little later, how would you
like to go back to the days of the Puritan Fathers,
those estimable old Liberals, who fled from England
because they were not there permitted to worship
according to their notions, and who immediately set
up just as intolerant a system in the land to which
they fled? It was all well enough for the Puritans;
but how was it with the Quakers, whom they exiled,
after making them harmless in disputations by bor-
ing their heretical tongues with orthodox hot irons?

"Or to go a little farther back, how would you
like to have the personal combat business restored?
That was a delightful practice, was n't it? A big
burly ruffian claimed your farm or abducted your
daughter; then the burly ruffian swore he was innocent, and demanded the trial by combat. He was
used to weapons, and his fighting weight was a hun-

dred and eighty-five : you never knew which end of
a sword to take hold of, and weighed one hundred
and twenty-five. But you had to do it. The first
round, down you went, and the judges declared him
innocent, and you guilty of bringing false accusations.
He kept the girl, and your head was chopped off, and
your property confiscated to the State. In those
good old days, the State meant the king and his pet
mistress. It is true there was a superstition that
Providence would protect the right; but, as a rule,
the burly ruffian in the wrong made short work of
the small man in the right.

"The thumb-screw, the rack, the stake, and all
that cheerful paraphernalia belonged to and was the
exclusive property of the good old times,— the good
old times that exiled the bold men who insisted that
the world was round and not flat, with other heresies.
Do you want them back again? You point at muni-
cipal and governmental corruption. I grant it bad
enough ; but bad as it is, it is better to have polite
thieves than brutal ones ; and it is a high compliment
to the times that the people are in possession of
property to be taxed. In your good old times,
the State and Church took it all as fast as it was
earned.

"It took the world thousands of years to get to
the point of civilization that would admit of a jury ;
and hundreds more to reach the sublime heights of a
republic. And it has just commenced at that. Both
have yet to be perfected.

"The mistake that men of your notions make is,

you don't seem to have any idea whatever that other men know anything or have any sense. Because a woman likes carpets on a floor better than rushes, is she less virtuous? Can't a man be as good, clad in decent broadcloth as in odorous sheep-skin? Is dirt akin to godliness, or does filth tend to enlarge the moral muscles? Could a man with a back-breaking sickle sing praises to the God of Nature any more melodiously than he can now, mounted on a comfortable reaper? Nay, my friend, on a reaper a man might thank Heaven he lived; with a sickle, I question whether he would feel that thankfulness.

"The more men know, the greater the inducement they have to virtuous life. In the barbarous age, before law was invented, if a man wanted a piece of land which another man claimed, the claimants met with stone hatchets. Both kept the land, — one of them on the surface, and the other some three feet beneath, with a hole in his head. As civilization progressed, the hatchet went out and law came in, and the more civilization we have the less hatchet we have. We have wars now, it is true; but it is because, and only because, we are not yet fully civilized. We have thieves and robbers now; but it is because there lurks yet in the human system a taint of the good old times. Civilization has not yet fully physicked humanity, and traces of barbarism remain. Napoleon was a varnished barbarian; Kaiser Wilhelm is an Attilla with veneering on. Then down in Delaware the whipping-post is a mile-stone in the path of the progress of the other States, useful merely to make the better people of other localities congratulate themselves on what they have surmounted.

"'Good old times,' forsooth! Go to, wretched man! To-day is the best day the world ever saw; to-morrow will be better, and its to-morrow better still. In five or ten thousand years, this world will be a tolerably decent place to live in. Do you know why men exposed their lives so recklessly in battle in your 'good old times'? Bravery! you say. Bosh! It was because there was nothing under heaven to live for; precisely as I, feeling that I must die some time, came to New Jersey, that I might leave this world without a pang of regret. It was a cowardly willingness to get out of the world, because there could be nothing worse.

"But leave me now. Instead of mourning for a miserable past, tackle the splendid present, and try to do something for a still more splendid future. Do something for the world you live in. Do something for the race you belong to. After hearing you talk, I might properly suggest that the best thing you could do for humanity would be to drown yourself; but I forbear. I am not in a sarcastic mood this morning. Go to! I am weary; leave me."

And the Sage went into his tent, and was soon in the arms of Morpheus.

XVII.

THE UTILITY OF DEATH.

ABOU BEN ADHEM was asked one day by a sorrowing man if there was n't a screw loose somewhere in the economy of nature, as regards the duration of life. " Why," asked this individual, ""why was Death permitted to come into the world at all ? "

Abou was never in so good humor as when he had an opportunity to moralize, and this was one not to be wasted. So he arranged himself in his easy-chair and got the man safely under his eye, and, as the Orientals say, " went for him."

" Death," said Abou, " is not to be catalogued among the evils of this world ; it is to be considered as the greatest blessing the world enjoys, and as the most useful of all the provisions of nature, — that is to say, when it is taken into account how men are made.

" If men were all as honest, as true, and as good as I am, for instance, Death could be dispensed with ; but as they are not, it is an absolute necessity as a great equalizer. It is the great balance-wheel and the great distributor. It is the bad rich man's check and the poor good man's protection; it is the salvation of the State and the hope of the individual.

"Listen to a brief history : —

"In Persia, a hundred years or more ago, lived Hogem. Hogem, in his youth, sailed a small schooner on the Gulf of Persia, from Koamud to Bangay. He accumulated dirhems, in a small way, at the business, for he allowed no competition. If another man started a schooner in the same trade, Hogem's craft always got to sailing wild, and was certain to collide with the new one, and burst a hole in her side and lay her up. Accidents of this kind got so frequent that no one cared to sail on Hogem's route, and he had the whole trade to himself.

" Of course, Hogem learned the advantage of having control of an entire trade, and he kept his eye out for it. When steam was introduced into Persia, he was the first to put on boats propelled by the new power, and he observed the same tactics that he did with his schooner, and of course made great piles of shekels by his steamboats.

" Then came railways, and Hogem kept his weather-eye cocked in that direction. He did not embark in railroads at the beginning, for he was talented. He waited till the people built them with their own money, and found they couldn't make them pay. He watched the road from Bangay to Koamud, the two most important cities in the Empire, and he waited his time. The road cost twenty millions of dirhems, but as it had never paid a dividend, the

stockholders were willing to sell at any price. So
Hogem bought a little over half of the stock, for little or nothing, to make himself President; then he
swindled the others out of their stock and owned it
all himself. It paid immediately, for he stopped all
the stealing, and the time had come when it was possible for the road to pay.

"Owning the road, he had a sure thing on the
people. They had to travel over it, and they were
compelled to use it to transport their produce, for
there was no other way for them. He put on just
such rates as he pleased, and he regarded their mur-
murs no more than the sighing of wind through rose-
bushes.

" The people murmured, and applied to the Council for relief. They said, in their Oriental way, ' Lo!
this Hogem has gobbled our railroad, and has us
where our hair is short. After other roads are built
he captures them, and we are helpless. Save us from
Hogem!'

"But Hogem laughed in his sleeve. 'Shall I let
this fat thing go out of my hands? What says Nig-
gah-mynstrel, the poet of the people?

> " When you have a good thing, save it, save it,
>   When you ketch a white cat, shave it, shave it —
>   When you ketch a white cat, shave it to de tail.'

These people are my white cats. Go to!'

" And he went to Teheran, where the Council met,
the same time that the representatives of the people
did; and he took gorgeous rooms at the Teheran

Hotel, and he put therein bottles of the juice of the grape and great jars of the strong waters of the Giaour, and tobacco cunningly rolled by the Espagnol, and he stored in his closet bags of dirhems.

" And then Hogem asked the members of the Council to visit him, and he gave to them the juice of the grape, and he warmed their hearts with strong waters. And as each went out, he took him aside and laid his finger beside his nose, saying, ' Here, take this bag of dirhems, for thou art a pleasant fellow, and a brick, and I love thee. And when my enemies, the people—whom may Allah confound !—come to the Council, and demand laws against my just charges for carrying their rice and things, say, " Go to ! Hogem is a good man and an honest man. His charges are just." And when the vote is taken, vote against them, and if you prevail, come to me again ; come alone, and there will be more strong waters — and perchance, haply, another bag of dirhems.'

" And Hogem put his finger to his nose, and winked a solemn wink of ineffable meaning, which was comprehended, for the member did likewise.

" Now, there were two hundred members of the Council, and the great man saw one hundred and five of them, and each, with a bag of dirhems under his robe, voted against the people. And straightway each of the one hundred and five had two bags of dirhems about him.

" Thus, you see, Hogem had the entire country at his mercy. He owned the Council so that it would not permit other roads to be built. In a little while he did not have to seek the members, for they sought him. They would say, 'If he has the gold, why should I not have my divvy?' Divvy is a Persian word, used in Councils, the meaning of which you, probably, do not understand.

"Now, here is where Death comes in to advantage. Hogem had all the Councils under his thumb; he was moving on the Shah himself; he would, in ten years more, have had all Persia at his feet: and you may imagine the condition we should have been in, with this one man as our sole ruler. Just as he was making a bigger and wickeder combination than ever, paralysis struck him and the people were saved. His combinations melted; his railroads had to be sold; competition came in, and things were again lovely in Persia.

"Suppose that the Frank, Bonaparte, had had eternal life. He would have gone on swallowing one nation after another, till he would have controlled the whole world. He would have met another Bonaparte, you say? Very good; that would have been worse, for the two would have kept the world at blood-letting forever.

"And then think of a world with such pests as George Francis Train and the Woodhull in it, with no prospect of relief from Death?

"'Good men die too.' Verily. But that does n't detract from the strength of my position a particle. For where there is one honest, or to put it stronger, where there is one man like myself, there are a thousand bad ones.

" The disparity between the two classes being so great, Death is an advantage. It is the safety-valve of society; it is the limit to human action; and as human action tends to the bad, why, the limit is an excellent good thing.

" When men all do right, probably there will be no more Death. But I really don't expect to ever see it. The man whose ancestors lived correctly and who lives correctly himself, lives longer than the one in whom these conditions do not exist. It is very likely that when the old virus is all out, that Death, which was intended as the cure for it, will go out with it. But as long as the virus is in, Death is necessary, as the cure for it. Poison spreads faster than wholesome things. A rum-mill will infect an entire neighborhood in half the time that a prayer-meeting can possibly convert it. Wickedness moves faster than an express train: goodness moves at the speed of the ox-cart.

" There are so many bad men, and disease is so slow, that I sometimes think there is a great deal of lightning squandered every year. With its quick action, its wonderful killing capacity, and so great a use for it, it is a thousand pities that more of it cannot be judiciously directed. But there are mysteries in nature.

" Were there no Death, what would the young woman married to an old man do, or the young man married to an old woman? Take offices where promotion comes by seniority. What anguish would wring the bosoms of the juniors if the seniors were immortal ! Death makes room for men ; Death checks the wicked, betters the condition of the good, — in short, it is altogether a sweet boon.

" My young friend, I long for Death ; for the next world, to a perfect man, can only be a blissful one. I long to go ! And now leave me."

" Stay !" said the young man, as he turned to go. " If you so long to go, why don't you go ? Death is attainable to any one."

"I continue to live," said Abou, " because I can do my fellow-men good by living."

And he walked slowly into his habitation.

XVIII.

A VISION OF THE HEREAFTER.

ABOU BEN ADHEM was annoyed one morning by an elderly gentleman, who desired to learn of the ideas the Persian Sage had of the Hereafter, particularly as to the style and quality of people who would be likely to reach a future of bliss.

Abou removed his chibouque from his lips, and moistening his throat with a long draught of sherbet, spoke to him thus : —

"My friend, many hundreds of years ago, when I was a comparatively young man, I dreamed one night that I had shuffled off this mortal coil, and was in the Land of the Hereafter. Methought I was decently deceased, had been genteelly buried, and a tomb-stone had been erected to my memory, on which were inscribed enough virtues to furnish a dozen. I blushed a spirit-blush when I read that tombstone, and dis-covered what an exemplary man I had been ; and I likewise wept a spirit-weep when I thought what a loss the world had sustained in my death.

"I ascended, and was knocking at the outer gate of Paradise for admittance. The season had been a very healthy one, for the National Convention of Physicians had been drowned while taking a steamboat excursion on the Persian Gulf, so the door-keeper had but little to do while my case was being decided. I whiled away an hour or two ascertaining the whereabouts of my old acquaintances, who had deceased during the ten years previous.

"'There is a large number of my friends up here?' I remarked, inquiringly.

"'Not very many,' was his reply.

"'Ebn Becar is here, I suppose?'

"'Not any Ebn Becar,' was the answer.

"'I am surprised,' I answered. 'Ebn Becar, the date-seller, not in Paradise! Be chesm, no man in Ispahan was more regular in his attendance at the mosque, and he howled his prayers like a dervish. He was exceedingly zealous in keeping the faithful in the line of duty.'

"'True,' said the door-keeper, 'true! But, you see, Ebn kept his eagle eye so intently fixed on his neighbor's feet that his own got off the road, and when he pulled up, it wasn't at the place he had calculated. His prayers were pleasing to a true believer; but as they were not backed up by doing things in proportion, they failed to pass current here.'

"'How fared it with Hafiz, the scribe? He was charitable; no man gave more to the poor than he.'

"'Hafiz did give many shekels to the poor each year, but it was the way he gave it that spoiled the effect of his charities. He gave, not for any love of his kind, but because it was a part of his system to give. He was afraid not to give. So he said, "I will answer the demands of the law of the Prophet by giving so much, which will ensure me Paradise," and fancied that was charity. When the widow of Selim, the mule-driver, employed him to save her inheritance to her children from her wicked brother, he required of her all that the law permitted him to exact, so that she said, " Lo ! I might as well have let my brother had the land." He answered, "The law gives it me. Go to ! " He would oppress the poor in a business way, and compromise with his conscience by subscribing a tenth of his profits to charity. Compromising never did work in such matters. The compromiser gives to the devil something of value, and receives in return that which damns him. The oppressions and graspings of Hafiz were exactly balanced, in number, by his charities; but as he died worth a million, the oppression side was the heaviest in quality. We keep books very accurately, you observe.'

"' Abdallah, the maker of shawls, is — '

"' No, he is n't. He was an ardent teacher of the rules the Prophet gave for the faithful, but he was the worst practiser I ever had any knowledge of. The strong waters of the Giaour ruined his prospects. He preached abstinence from wine, but he constantly partook of the forbidden drink. He loved wine, and immediately proceeded to deceive himself into the belief that he had dyspepsia and had to take it. Hearing once that strong liquor was an antidote for the bite of a serpent, he absolutely moved into a province where serpents abounded, and went out regularly to get bitten. He talked loudly against gluttony, but excused himself for eating five courses by holding that he needed it to keep himself up. He succeeded in deceiving himself, but he could n't deceive us.'

"'Kahkani, the poet, whose songs were all in praise of virtue, is here? The fervent goodness that produced such morality must be safe!'

"'Quite wrong, my dear sir. Kahkani's poems were beautiful; but bless you! he never felt the sentiments expressed in them. He had an itching for fame, and writing spiritual hymns happened to be his best hold. If he could have written comic songs better than hymns, he would have written comic songs.'

"'Whom have you here, pray?'

"'Saadi, the camel-shoer, is here.'

"'Saadi! why, he was constantly violating the law of the Prophet.'

"True! he would even curse the camels he was shoeing. But he was always sorry for it, and he would mourn over the infirmities of his temper, and strove honestly and zealously all the time to live better and be better. He did not make a great success, but he did the best he could. He gave liberally of his substance, without blatting it all over Ispahan. When he gave a dirhem, he did n't pay the newspapers two dirhems to make the fact public, which is my definition of genuine charity. Then there's Firdusi, the carpet-cleaner —'

"'He never gave anything.'

"'Certainly not, for he had nothing to give. The Prophet never asked impossibilities. He would have given if he had had it, and he tried hard to get it. Then there's Jelal-ed-din —'

"'He couldn't make a prayer.'

"'True! but he said "Amen" to those who could, and he meant it, which was more than half those who made the prayers could say.'

"'And Wassaf, the teacher, — where is he? A more pure and blameless life no man ever led!'

"'He is here, but occupies a very low place.'

"'A low place?'

"'Verily. Wassaf did not sin, it is true; but it was no credit to him that he did not. A more egregiously deceived man never lived or died. He obeyed the laws of the Prophet, because he could not do otherwise, thus crediting himself with what he could not avoid. He could not be a glutton, for his stomach was weak; he could not partake of the strong waters of the Frank, because his brain would not endure it; he was virtuous, because he was too cold-blooded, too thin-blooded, to have any passion. He had not moral force enough to commit a decent sin, and this inability to be wicked he fancied was righteousness. He was a moral oyster. He, an iceberg, plumed himself upon being cold. Now Agha, the flute-player, who was at times a glutton and a wine-bibber, and all the rest of it, is several benches higher than Wassaf. For Agha's blood boiled like a cauldron; he was robust, he had the appetite of the rhinoceros

of the Nile, and a physical nature that was constantly
pushing him to the commission of sin; but Ágha,
feeling, knowing that it was wrong, fought against it
manfully. He fell frequently, for the Evil One knew
his weak moments; but he rose and fought against
himself, and managed to come out victor, at least
half the time. There was no more merit in Wassaf's
virtue than there is in an iceberg's being cold. But
for a burning volcano like Agha to keep himself
down to an even temperature, that was great.

"'My friend, it is not worth while to enumerate,
but — well, you will know more when you get inside,
if you *do* get inside. You have seen the sky-rockets
of Jami. They ascend with much fizz, and make a
beautiful show, but alas! before they reach the skies
they explode, and disappear in a sheet of flame. Precisely so with many men. They soar aloft on their
professions; but they, too (to use a vulgarism), bust
before they attain Paradise, and go down in a sheet
of flame.

"'The true believer, who practises what he believes,
is an arrow. Pointed with belief, feathered with
works, death shoots him off; he pierces the clouds
and lands on the right side of the river.'

"At this point," continued Abou, "I awoke. My
ideas of the future I got largely from that vision.
My opinion is that in New Jersey, as in Persia, there
are a great many people deceiving themselves. Go
thy way! Be virtuous and be happy. I would rest
me."

XIX.

REMORSE: THE NATURE OF THE AVERAGE ARTICLE.

ABOU BEN ADHEM, in an unpleasant frame of mind, one morning, was approached by a long-nosed, sad-looking man, who propounded to him the query, " What is Remorse? "

To which Abou replied, " The humiliating sense of an abject failure."

" What! " exclaimed the seeker after truth, " is there no such thing as sorrow and regret for wrong-doing? "

" Frequently, my aged infant, frequently. There are minds so susceptible to proper impressions, so spiritualized, if I may use the expression, as to feel a pang or two after they have done a wrong thing; but they are not common.

" Listen to my own experience. A great many years ago, in Persia, I made the acquaintance of a party of men who met frequently to indulge in a game played with cards, which, I presume, you know nothing of here, called, in Persia, drah-poquier. It is a curious game. The cards are dealt one at a time, till each has five; then those who are playing, put on the centre of the table a coin, such as has been determined upon — say a kopeck; then they are allowed to throw up as many cards as they choose, taking from the pack an equal number; then the man who sits next to the dealer remarks sarcastically, 'I am the aged one, impoverish me,' and the betting begins. It is a curious game and a fluctuating, the players being kept in a pleasant state of uncertainty as to what the others have, till they come to what they call a 'show-down.'

"Well, I learned this game, and played it with unvarying success for some days, winning, on an average, four or five dirhems at a sitting. As I gathered in my spoils I saw nothing wrong in the game. It seemed to me a most desirable and, in all respects, a gentlemanly game.

"'I am sorry,' I said to myself, 'for Hafiz, the bellows-maker, and for Nadir, the seller of shawls; but Allah knows I risk my substance on the cards as do they, and had they my luck they would have my money. Be chesm, it is a highly moral game, and had I an hundred children I would teach it them. What is there wrong in it? It is my money which I risk; it is their money which they risk. There is no trickery or cheating in this game, for the cards are fairly dealt, and we make wagers on our judgment or our luck. So does the merchant who buys the wheat of Khurdistan, believing that the crop will be short, and that it will go up. So does the merchant who sells the corn of Kohmul, believing that the crop will be heavy and the price will go down.

What is this but gambling? If they play with wheat
and corn, why should not Hafiz and I play with
cards? And then it strengthens the mind, it develops the judgment, quickens the reasoning powers,
and broadens, widens, and strengthens the mental
man. It is a noble game and a great pursuit.'

" Thus reasoned I, joyously.

" I had no remorse, nor did it occur to me that it
was gambling.

" But one night it so happened that I had a certainty on Hafiz. I had three cards alike in my hand,
— that is to say, three aces, — and when the cards
were helped, as the phrase is, I took another. Hafiz
drew one card to the four that he held, and the betting
began. Now, four aces is a strong hand, there being
but one that can beat it, namely, a strate-phlush. I
wagered a kopeck to help Hafiz on to his ruin. How
I gloated over those four aces! I saw nothing wrong
in those four aces, nor in making out of Hafiz, the
bellows-mender, all that he should make by his trade
for a year. He saw my modest kopeck and said he
would wager a dirhem in addition. Exulting in the
strength of my four aces, I gladly put up the dirhem,
and remarked that such was my faith in my hand
that I would impoverish him to the extent of ten
dirhems more. Hafiz — on whose head light curses!
— saw the ten dirhems, and boosted me (boosted is a
Persian phrase) one hundred dirhems. I made sure
that the four aces was not an optical delusion, and
went him one thousand dirhems, which he saw, and
came back at me five thousand dirhems, which, feel-

ing that it would be cruel to utterly ruin him, I called without further gymnastics.

"Smilingly I laid down my four aces and reached for the property. Smilingly he put away my out-stretched and eager hand, and laid down beside my four aces his accursed hand, which was a strate-phlush.

"'The property is mine?' said he.

"'It is!' said I.

"Then I experienced a feeling of remorse. Then I felt that drah-poquier was gambling, and that gamb-ling in any form was a sin of the most heinous na-ture, and that I had been guilty of a crime.

"'Oh, why,' I exclaimed 'did I ever permit my-self to become infatuated with the desire for gam-ing! If I win, it is my neighbor's dirhems; if I lose, it is my own. In any case, there is nothing of actual value that passes. While we use capital in gambling, we produce nothing. One side is richer, the other poorer, and there has been a waste of precious time. Besides, it is terribly demoralizing. It infatuates a man and enfeebles his mind. His mind dwells on the game to the exclusion of every-thing that is good; it crushes out everything that is high and noble, and develops everything that is mean and small in one's nature. It ruins the loser financially and ruins the winner morally. Wretch that I am! why did I ever permit myself to play at all? Why did I permit this cursed infatuation to grip me?'

"And Remorse sat on me, and I beat my breast

and pulled my hair. Bewailing my wickedness, I determined to purge myself of the unholy thing.

" Would I have so thought and so done had I held the strate-phlush, and the accursed bellows-mender the four aces? I do not know.

" Once more. In my youth I drank deep of pleasure. The wines of Shiraz were not too good for me, and the strong waters of the Frank I indulged in to a degree that was astonishing. I had a constitution of iron, and the endurance of an army mule. I could drink all night and disport myself all day. There seemed to be no limit to it. Moralists said it was wicked, but I laughed. What cared I for the moralists? ' Go to ! ' I said, ' life is short and it behooves me to get the most out of it. A fig for your preachers and your preaching ! Wine is good — I will drink it. The black-eyed woman pleases me — I will enjoy her society. The rattle of the dice is music to mine ear — they shall rattle.' Pleasure I wanted, pleasure I enjoyed, and I went for it in every possible form. The moments flew by rapidly, each one bringing with it a fresh delight; the days sped by, each one crowned with a new pleasure.

" But finally it came to an end. My stomach gave out and dyspepsia set in. I could drink no more of the rich wines or of the strong waters; women pleased me not; the rattle of the dice was no longer a pleasure : for I was, to use a Persian phrase, played out. My system gave out all at once. I had hunted pleasure, and pleasure was now hunting me. I had lived out my vitality, but time remained.

"Then I experienced what is called remorse. With dyspepsia gnawing at my stomach; with my knees weakened and my back of no account whatever; incapable of what had delighted me, and diseased in every part, I was sorry I had lived the life I had lived. Not because the Koran interdicted it, not because the life had been of itself wrong, but because certain pains and penalties followed the life which gave me more pain than the life had given me pleasure. So long as my health lasted I cared nothing for the violation of the precepts; it was only when the penalties were enforced that I felt a sorrow for what I had done.

"There are men — and women — who do, I presume, experience a genuine remorse for the commission of wrongs, great and small; but, as I said, the number is small. It is the penalties that hurt them. Solomon, of whom you have probably heard, did not say "vanity of vanities," so long as he was in good health and could sin with some zest. It was only after he was old and incapable that remorse struck him. Precisely so it is with the most of us. When the candle of enjoyment is all burned out, and the dark, black snuff alone remains, we look at it with regret and remorse. Possibly, it may be grief at the sin, but as a rule, methinks, it is grief because we cannot do it over again, or because now that we have the penalties to pay, that it did not pay to do it at all."

"But — "

"Don't say another word. You have got all out

of me that is necessary for yóu to know. In fact, as I have spoken, you have got all that there is in the topic. Leave me."

And the Sage went wearily in to his breakfast.

XX.

A LESSON FOR HUSBANDS.

ABOU BEN ADHEM was asked one day by a
seeker after knowledge whether a man had better marry or not.

The Sage was in a good mood for talk: he had
had his supper and it suited him, the tobacco in
his chibouque was precisely to his taste, and he had
made a fair operation that day in stocks.   Life was
to him more than usually pleasant, and being in
good humor he was disposed to narrate.

"Listen," said he, "to a true tale.

"I was once a married man — possibly I am yet.
The lady whom I married was too sinewy and tough
to die in a hurry.

"If I sigh as I speak let not that sigh be interpreted
as an indication that I am an unbeliever in matrimony.

"Matrimony in the abstract is a good and desirable thing; whether it is *always* a good thing is another
question.

"I shall not testify, for I cannot be an unprejudiced
witness.   I was married and I am bald-headed.   It
was not a fever that took out my hair; it came out

suddenly one night during an argument with my wife.

"When two people — of opposite sex of course — discover that their hearts throb in unison, they should be joined, that they may continue to so throb. When two people — a man and a woman — discover that their tastes are similar, likewise their hopes and aims, they should marry. In such cases life is, doubtless, a rose-tinted dream.

"But where the masculine person is not tremendously strong, is timid in his nature, and addicted to miscellaneous pleasures; and the female member of the firm is five feet nine inches in height, addicted to having her own way, and very strong in the arm, I will not say that, for the man at least, marriage is a good thing. I do not believe it. I have had experiences. There is such a thing as will power: a strong will in a weak body will bear down and override a weak will in a strong body; but when the strong will animates a strong body the combination is fearful. Give the wife both these qualities, and it is bad for the husband. The husbands of such wives must be exceedingly mild in temper to retain their hair. I have known many men who possess such wives, and have noticed that they invariably wore wigs. But for such wives a worthy trade would languish. How the lines of life cross each other! Who would suppose that temper had anything to do with the trades? Life is a riddle.

"Possibly it is bad for the wife when the husband is so constituted, but I know not. I am speaking from the standpoint of the husband, and am in no mood for pursuing the theme further than is necessary.

"I am large enough, and am not exactly timid, but I am, or rather was, of an easy, quiet, philosophical nature. I was wont to submit to almost anything rather than have a struggle. Struggles I detested. My wife, Zulieka, was five feet nine inches in height, and not timid. The roar of the lion, though he was behind iron bars, would frighten me : she would stride into his den and conquer him. She was eminently fitted by nature to be a lion-tamer in a moral menagerie ; and when I read that lions did sometimes rend their keepers into infinitesimal fragments, I frequently wished that she would embrace that profession.

"I have described my late wife, Zulieka, and her husband, myself. I put them in the order in which they stood before the world.

"My married life was not altogether a summer morn.

"Dark tempests frequently arose and swept over our domestic hearth. Zulieka represented, in these tempests, the thunder, lightning, wind, and hail, and I the worn, beaten, and drenched traveller on the dreary moor.

"Zulieka had a passion for control ; she felt that she was born to command, and she did command everybody who came near her, from the date of her birth. When she put her foot down, it came down with most significant emphasis ; when she said anything, she generally intended to be distinctly understood as meaning it. Two of her younger sisters committed suicide to escape her domination.

"I did not willingly propose to this superior being: she captured me; I was taken by her. She forced me to propose to her, and compelled me to ask the consent of her father. When she got her eye on me and told me to do this I no more dared to disobey her than I would have dared to face a hungry tiger. I was her property, she had taken me, — and I yielded.

"Never shall I forget the expression of satisfaction, of devout thankfulness, that illuminated the countenance of that long-suffering father when I asked for her. 'Take her, my son, take her, and *we'll* be happy.' It was a slight departure from the regular formula, but I did not observe it. I thought him liberal when he furnished me the means to start in business, and insisted upon fixing the location himself.

"It was a thousand miles from where he lived, and so remote from railroads that Zulieka could never visit the home of her childhood, and there revive the sweet recollections of the past. It was in the cold, mountainous North. Was it accident or design? Alas! what conundrums life continually presents for solution, and to how many of them do we reply, 'I give it up'!

"My only hope of release was that cholera or yellow fever or some exceedingly fearful disease would strike her. It would take cholera or yellow fever to do for her; her great nature would laugh the severe bilious or the more grasping typhoid to scorn. *Cerebro-spinal meningitis* might bring her, but I doubted it. My chief trust was in cholera and yellow fever. They are sudden in action, and might surprise her.

"I awaited anxiously the advent of those cheerful liberators. 'But they might take you!' I knew that. But I had the advantage of her. Life was desirable to her so long as she had the ecstasy of banging me. Life was of no account to me so long as she lived to bang. Therefore, I sighed for the advent of yellow fever or cholera.

"I did thrice attempt to combat this terrible woman. My first effort was a failure. The succeeding ones were likewise. I well remember my first essay. I attempted to dictate something to her concerning our child, Hakao. She hurled one look at me. Oh, that look! It was sufficient. I acknowledged her power from that moment.

"We had been wedded five years. I longed to be my own man, — to taste the ecstasy of doing just once as I should see fit. I determined to do it. 'I am a man,' I said to myself, 'and she is a woman. I will assert my manhood.'

"That very evening, as I took my copote after tea to go out, Zulieka remarked, —

"'Abou, you will be home by half-past eight.'

"I drew myself up to my full height (five feet seven), and assuming my sternest look, replied, —

"'Zulieka, I shall not be at home at half-past eight. It may be half-past nine, half-past ten, half-past eleven, or perchance daylight. I shall stay out as long as I choose, and return when I please. I am a man, madam, and not a child.'

"Zulieka started up as if to annihilate me, but a second thought struck her, and she subsided, with the remark, 'Very well, Abou, very well.'

"She was quiet and apparently resigned. My boldness had quelled her. Her face was quiet but cold.

"So the ice of a lake is quiet and cold, but there is death in the chilly waters under it.

"But I had embarked in this crusade and determined to follow it, let it end where it would, and I put on my copote with emphasis and left the house.

"That evening I met several of my friends, from whom I had been for some time estranged by the severe rule of my spouse. We had a supper, and, after appropriate beverages, cards and cigars. My friends were all married men, all possessed of — no, not of, but by — muscular wives, and they determined to enjoy the liberty they had stolen.

"I said supper and beverages. The supper was light; the beverages were not. We drank lustily, talked first loudly, then huskily, then sillily, and finally at two o'clock in the morning separated, vowing to meet at the same place every night. Each wended his serpentine way to his respective home. Crooked are the paths of life — at two in the morning.

"I found my way to my home easily enough. It was a modest cottage in the suburbs, in the centre of a very respectable lot of ground. I should have preferred a house nearer the centre of the town: Zulieka doted on nature, and so we had a small garden, with a lawn, clipped trees, worms, bugs, and things of that sort.

"I found my way to the door, but not through it. I should always have preferred to carry a night-key, but Zulieka preferred that I should not. Hence I did not.

"'Locked out!' muttered I to myself. 'Thank you, my dear. I shall essay the window. Keep me out of my own house? Ha! ha!' And I laughed derisively.

"I tried the windows, but they were all securely locked. The skilful burglar might have essayed those windows in vain. He would have had his labor for his pains.

"It was a bitter cold night, and in parting with my friends I had forgotten my overcoat. There I stood shivering in the wind, while Zulieka was warm and snug in bed. Loudly I knocked, — only echo answered.

"All the windows? No! I bethought me of one which I had not tried. I disliked additions to a house, but Zulieka preferred them; and therefore an addition to our house had been built. It was a laundry, — a one-story structure in the rear of the kitchen, with one window in it. That window I tried, and to my infinite joy it was unfastened. 'Ha! ha! From the laundry to the kitchen, from the kitchen to the dining-room, thence to the sitting-room, and thence, — ha! ha!'

" And I pondered as to whether I should smother her with pillows, as Othello did Desdemona, and I doubted as to whether I would give her time to say her prayers. I remember now that I finally resolved that it would be only fair to give her time to say one short one.

" Carefully I hoisted the window, and holding it up with one hand clambered up. Poising myself on the sill, I sprang gayly, not upon the floor, but into a barrel of ice-cold water, which had been carefully placed directly under that window, by whose loving hands I had no difficulty in determining. With a howl of anguish I struggled to get out, and in so doing I tipped the barrel over.

" Soaked thoroughly, and with my teeth chattering like castanets, I rushed to the door that opened into the kitchen. It was locked. The window! I would climb out the aperture through which I came, and hie me to a hotel. Woe was me! the window had fallen, and had fastened itself so that I could not open it. I was a prisoner in a laundry, eight feet square, the thermometer at the freezing point, wet through and through, with no prospect of getting out.

" ' I will sleep,' I said, and lay down. Alas! the same kind hand that had locked all the doors, and all the windows but one, and had placed a barrel of water under that one, had likewise poured several barrels on the floor. The floor was a good one and held water, and there was at least three inches of that fluid on it, in which I lay down.

" Springing to my feet I leaned for rest against the

wall. The cold increased in intensity every minute, and in an hour I was sheathed in an armor of ice, and was as stiff and incapable of motion as the Cardiff Giant.

" My tongue was the only member of my body that was free, and that I employed in hurling anathemas at Zulieka, who was warm and comfortable in her bed. If she finally goes to the place to which I consigned her that night, she will be as much too warm as I was then too cold.

" Need I continue the harrowing tale? How slowly dragged along the hours! The clock struck two. Two! Why, five hours must pass before seven, and could I endure till then? Three! four! five! I was gradually congealing. Life was leaving me slowly. I was not altogether miserable nor wholly discontented with my fate. Should I die and be compelled to meet the King of Pandemonium himself I could not be much worse off. Life with Zulieka had robbed death of its terrors. As I thought of her I exclaimed, ' O Death, where is thy sting?'

" Morning did come at last. At 7 A. M. Zulieka arose, the first of the household. She sang her matin song gayly as she dressed. I yelled like a Camanche. Cheerfully she came to me. On her face was an expression of pity and surprise.

" ' Why, Abou,' said this female, with her large eyes wide open, ' can this be you? Where, oh where have you been all night? I waited till very late for you, and then went to bed, and lay uneasy all night fearing that something had happened to you. Bless me ! you are wet through and through, and your clothes are frozen stiff.   Dear me !'

"And she looked as innocent as — I pause for a simile.   A stranger would not have supposed that she planned the trap into which I had fallen, and was laughing internally at her success.

"'Take me down,' I replied, 'and lay me in front of the grate.'

"She did so, and as I was thawing out, she put her arms about my neck and exclaimed, —

"'Dearest, how cruel it was in you to stay all night away from your Zulieka !'

"I made no reply, — there was none to make.

"I may live long or I may die soon.   The rheumatism I am enjoying at this time, and the cough which is rending me, I charge to that night.   But long or short I never contested the field with Zulieka again.   I was no match for her.   I might as well have engaged Mr. Heenan in the roped arena, or attempted to cope with Prof. Agassiz in corals and things.   She was my superior.   I was down.   Had I arisen I should have been knocked down again. I spared her the trouble and myself the humiliation. I stayed where I was.   My only satisfaction was that before I left her she went back to her father.   That was my revenge for his failing to rescue me from her.

"My story is done.   I do not know whether it bears upon the question you put to me or not, for I have really forgotten the question.   Had I remembered the question, I should have varied the narrative so that it would have been a complete answer.

"But you must be an incomprehensible idiot if you cannot get a moral out of anything I say. Go!"

And Abou relighted his chibouque and composed himself for a long reverie.

XXI.

THE SHORTEST ROAD TO FAME.

THERE came to Abou ben Adhem one day a young man who insisted upon being put in the way to the achievement of distinction. Abou looked the young man over with great care, and proceeded to give him a prescription at once.

"There are various kinds of fame, my son," said the Sage, "but to attain any one of them requires an adaptability to that particular one, and much labor. It takes a great many years to attain eminence at the bar — that is, as a lawyer; political distinction is attained only by years of labor; and the same may be said of the pulpit and the tripod. From the size and peculiar shape of your head, I should say that your shortest cut to fame is *via* the practical joke. It is not the best reputation to have and hold, but it will answer you, because it strikes me you are fitted for it. The practical joker may, in a year's time, become sufficiently famous to have the town all speaking of "Jones's last good thing," if Jones gives his whole mind to it, and has nothing else to take his attention.

12

A few plain directions are all that are necessary.

"In the first place, a practical joker should have a good income, — indeed, he ought to be rich. If he is rich enough to be always able to order and pay for wine, dinners, and carriages, he can always be sure of having in his train a regiment of 'good fellows,' who will repeat his good things, and who will frown down the sober people, who, if left to themselves, would howl down the fountain of all their joys as an unmitigated nuisance, and a pest only a trifle less terrible than a mad dog.

"Secondly. The practical joker must give his entire attention to the pursuit, for one effort, though it be successful, will not hold permanent distinction. It must be repeated daily, till the public shall hear as regularly of "Jones's (we will say) last" as they do of bank defalcations.

"Thirdly. The practical joker must have no weak scruples. The feelings of others must not affect him, nor must any earthly consideration turn him from his purpose.

"He need not have wit or originality; all that is necessary is stolidity, and money enough to keep his corps of followers to applaud and repeat.

"Having designated the qualities necessary for success in this pursuit, I shall suggest a few practical jokes which have done good service in their day, and will do to use again.

"We will suppose that A., the practical joker, has a friend, B., who lives during the summer at Staten Island. B. has a brother in Chicago. What more

exquisite piece of fun could there be than to
have A. forge a telegram to B., in the name of the
clerk of, say the Fifth Avenue Hotel, to the effect
that his brother fell with a stroke of paralysis in the
corridor of the hotel, just as he was registering his
name, and was at the point of death? B., seeing the
name all right, and not suspecting that that funny
dog, A., had anything to do with it, would be greatly
distressed. He would tear away from table, throw
himself on the ferry-boat, frantically call a carriage,
ride like a madman to the Fifth Avenue, and rush
to the office and excitedly demand the room where
his brother was dying. At this point A. and his crowd
should appear, and, laughing till their sides ache at
the blank wonderment of the clerk, and the distressed expression of B., should shout "Sold!" Nothing could be more exquisitely humorous than this.
Every practical joker should thank me for the suggestion. I do not say that it is above the average of
practical jokes, but it is a trifle different from the
usual run. Then it is capable of infinite variety. A
man has many relatives, and it could be run on him
for all of them. Thus to one it might be telegraphed
that his wife was dying, his father, his mother, his
son in West Point, his daughter in Vassar, and so
forth.

"If a man has a maiden aunt, from whom he has
expectations, what could be better than to telegraph
him of her death, and let things go to the length of
ordering mourning? How glorious it would be to
have the pleasure of poking him in the ribs for a

month, with the query, "How is your aunt? Ha!
ha! ha!"

"Another 'good thing' is to issue tickets of invita-
tion to an amateur performance at some hall for the
benefit of a charity, and to prescribe full dress for
the occasion. It is better always to select for such a
"rig," a rainy season, that the "victims" of the
"sell" may be put to as much trouble and expense
as possible. If three thousand invitations are issued,
and the printing is well done, it is safe to assume
that two thousand five hundred will attend. What
rare sport to see two thousand five hundred ladies
and gentlemen get out of carriages, only to find a
dark hall! This was done in New York once; but
the joke was not carried half far enough. The joker
was a poor one, and did not extract half the juice
from it that was possible. To have made it complete,
he should have employed boys to stand in the dark,
and bespatter the ladies' dresses with mud, as they
alighted from their carriages and got back into them.
To have armed the boys with squirt-guns, that they
might shower the ladies with water from the gutters,
would have been a positive triumph of genius. But
to have simply thrown the mud would have been a
proper and sufficiently humorous finish.

"The trick of advertising a 'dog wanted' at the
house of a friend is very good. But few things can
be funnier than the perplexity of the lady of the
house indicated in the advertisement, as the regi-
ments of ragamuffins come with dogs in their arms.
So, likewise, is the advertising that a man will fly

from the top of Trinity Church, particularly if you designate the man funnily, as, for instance, 'Herr Sellemall,' or 'Monsieur Foolemall,' or any appellation of the kind. These names are easy of construction, as will be seen, and when the fact works through the heads of the expectant crowd that the German 'Herr Sellemall' is in English 'sell-'em-all,' the way they shout, 'Sold, by Jove!' is a reward that practical jokers always appreciate.

"Another exceedingly pleasant practical joke is to stretch a cord across a gateway to a church, Sunday night, at an elevation of say five feet eight inches. As the congregation pass out under the cord, it neatly takes off and ruins the hats of all under that height, and rasps the faces of all over that altitude. The fright of an ancient maiden lady of attenuated proportions, as the cord strikes her face and breaks the skin on her nose and cheeks, is very amusing. The effect of this is immensely heightened by stretching another stout cord across the gateway at an elevation from the ground of say a foot, just high enough to trip them as they pass. Nothing can be more exquisitely funny than to see their consternation at the first cord, unless it is to see them sprawling in the mud over the second.

"There are other jokes fitted to all, but there is a class on which only medical students should venture. For instance, it is a 'big thing' to invite a party of friends to drink, and dexterously to get into their glasses a few drops of croton oil, or to substitute tartar emetic for cream of tartar in the kitchen of a

friend, that it may get into the cake served for re-
freshments at a party. One rare wag whom I knew
once in the most dexterous manner put some coal-oil
in the lemonade, at a little gathering given by a
clergyman's wife, and he and the few choice spirits
who were ' in it ' got no end of fun out of the distress
of the hostess and the disgust of the guests. The
circumstance created trouble in the parish, which re-
sulted in the dismissal of the minister; but that was
nothing : the faces of the people who got a taste of
that coal-oil were ludicrous beyond description.

" A pin stuck in the bottom of a chair, in which a
precise old lady is to sit down, is a good thing, as is
also the tieing of two cats, and slinging them across
your neighbor's fence, under his window.

" In fact, there is no limit to the amusement that
can be got out of this kind of thing. Sewing up the
sleeves of a friend's coat, when he is in a hurry to
get to a train, is a most exquisite performance, and
to blacken the face of a sleeping man is a piece
of humor that always affords the liveliest satisfaction.

" And the beauty of this kind of humor, the
great advantage in it is, it is as applicable to animals
as to men. A dog may be made the source of much
amusement. It is the nature of dogs when they approach each other to put their noses together, which
is equivalent, we presume, to the hand-shaking of
humans. Now, the practical joker who inserts a pin
in the muzzle of his dog does a very bright thing.
The dog will run the pin into the noses of all the

dogs who salute him, and the howls of the punctured
canines, and the look of blank astonishment on the face
of the innocent cause of the trouble, afford amusement
beyond expression. Tieing a tin kettle to a dog's tail
is another good thing. The frightened dog, at full
speed, will charge into a crowd of persons, and scatter them in a highly amusing manner. I have known
ladies to faint, and horses to be frightened so that
they ran away, and an immense number of exceedingly ludicrous incidents to happen in consequence.

"Another amusing trick may be played with a dog.
Buy a large Newfoundland, — a very shaggy one,
whose coat of hair will hold a barrel of water; then
invite a party of your friends to the water-side. The
ladies should be dressed in white, and the gentlemen,
also, in light pantaloons. Throw a stick into the
water, and say, 'Get it, Nero!' Then get into the
centre of the group. The sagacious dog will swim
out and get the stick, and will rush back to you, and
rub against all who stand in his way; and when he
gets to you he will shake himself, and completely
drench the whole party, and soil their clothes. If
the water is muddy the effect of the joke will be
heightened very much.

"In short, there are a thousand ways of doing this
kind of thing, and the advantage is that anybody can
do it. And it is safe, too; for you do not practise it
on anybody but your friends. If you should 'get
off' a practical joke on a stranger he might knock
you down; but your friend, no matter how much
annoyed he might be, would never do it. He will

swear and howl about it; but you laugh at him, and get mirth even out of his anger.

"Some people are unreasonable enough to speak of practical jokers as 'nuisances,' as 'pests,' and so forth, and possibly they are right. There are those so utterly devoid of the sense of fun that they object to be put to serious inconvenience, or to bodily hurt, or to be made to appear ridiculous for the sake of making amusements for others. But such people should not be regarded. The practical joker has his point to make, — he wants to rise a little above the level, and this is the only way in which he can do it. Therefore, it should not be barred to him, and those who growl should be frowned down. But one who has nothing else to do can well afford to bear this stigma for the amusement and reputation he gets.

"I have shown you, my ambitious young friend, how you may attain distinction. Go, and attain it! Be bold and merciless. The few who have sought to climb to eminence and have failed have fallen because they were not bold and had scruples. Go, my son, go!"

The young man left the presence, and Abou reclined on his divan and laughed heartily.

"By the bones of the Prophet!" he chuckled to himself, "this morn have I done humanity some service. That young man will attempt this kind of thing in his native State of New Jersey, whose people will refuse to see anything good in it. His eyes will be blackened on his first attempt, his sec-

ond will procure his being dragged through a horse-
pond, and his third will be the means of his dying
prematurely.   Then will the world be the better for
my advice.   Bismillah, it is good!"

And the Sage laughed himself to sleep.

XXII.

THE HISTORY OF ZODIAC, QUEEN OF PERSIA.

ABOU BEN ADHEM, the Sage, was reposing in
his tent early in the beautiful month of September. The frosts had tinted the maples, showering
their summits with glory; the green of the pines,
intensified by the touch of the forerunner of the
winter king, made a gorgeous contrast with the
purple and scarlet and gold in which the other trees
were robed; and the air, crisp as well as balmy, with
skies clear and beautiful, made a combination sufficiently satisfying to make a well-balanced person glad
that he lived, and that he lived on this much ma-
ligned earth.

While resting on his divan and enjoying his chibouque, a stranger raised the cloth of his tent, and
without ceremony, entered.

"Why this intrusion?" demanded Abou, angrily.
"By the bones of the Prophet, shall not the true believer have his rest? Shall a man be disturbed in his
reveries without a why or a wherefore? Who art
thou, unmannered man?"

"Mighty Abou," replied the unabashed stranger,

"I come for advice. Advice is what I want and what I will have. If I get it no other way, I shall pump it out of you. I shall hold you here by the button-hole till what I want you can give. You cannot escape me."

Abou resigned himself to his fate. It was a leading principle in the philosophy of that great man that —

"What can't be cured, love,
Must be endured, love,"

And he carried it out religiously.

"State your case, my pod-auger, state your case. I will beam on the pathway of your troubles. State your case."

"Mighty Abou," said the stranger, "I have a lady friend who has ducats. She is the possessor of great stores of gold and silver, and has lands and tenements without number. We have been engaged to be married for a year, and when that marriage is consummated I shall have something to say about those effects, which my soul yearns for. She is sixty-three, and as ugly as original sin, but I love her —"

"Estate," interpolated Abou, softly.

"As never man loved," continued the stranger.

"Why don't you marry her?"

"She is whimsical. Whenever I urge her to name the day, she says love is a hollow dream, and remarks that she longs to be an angel and with the angels stand. In brief, she threatens to commit suicide and leave a heartless world, and I think she means to do it. Twice have I held her when she threatened to throw herself out of the window; thrice have I wrenched from her grasp the deadly laudanum; and times without number have I saved her from self-destruction by other means. I am compelled to watch her perpetually, and I am, as you see, worn to a shadow by anxiety. If she would marry me I should not be so particular as to her notions of self-destruction, for she could not take with her lands and personal property; but to have her kill herself before that property passes to me! It is too sad to think of."

Abou sat for a moment in deep reverie. Then he spoke : —

" Listen to a tale of ancient Persia.

" Zodiac, the queen, had reached the mature age of sixty-three. She was not as beautiful as an houri ; on the contrary, she was as ugly as a red barn in my native State of Ma — that is, my native province of Koamud. At that age she got into her head the idea that it would be better for her and her people, more especially for herself,— for in Persia, as in other countries, the potentates count themselves more carefully than they do their people, — that she should go into the great silent Hereafter, which she prepared to do by throwing herself from the top of the east tower of the royal palace. As that structure was nine hundred and sixty-three feet high, the chances were that if she ever took that leap she would be injured fatally, and she would cease being queen with great suddenness.

"Now, Nadir-el-din, the grand vizier, did not

like this whim of the venerable queen, for her
nephew, who would succeed to the throne, hated him,
and would inevitably depose him and chop off his
head immediately thereafter, — a procedure which
grand viziers especially object to. But how to
prevent it was the question. He had restrained her
by various pretexts for a year, until finally Zodiac
informed him one day, that on the next morning, at
precisely nine, she should hurl herself from the tower
positively without reserve; there was no use of
further talk about it, and there should be no post-
ponement on account of weather. It had to be done.

"A happy thought struck Nadir-el-din, — a very
happy thought. He had twenty-four hours, and
nations and grand viziers have been frequently saved
in that time. He summoned the court dressmaker,
and ordered her to make for the queen a dress of
unparalleled magnificence.

"'Spare no expense,' he said. 'Let the material
be of the richest, and the work on it the most exquisite. Let diamonds and pearls and amethysts
and emeralds blaze and shine and glitter all over it.
And have it done by to-morrow at seven, or off goes
your head! Now throw yourself!' he said, relaps-
ing into the imaginative style of the dreamy East.

"The dressmaker shuddered, for the time was short;
but when a head is at stake almost anything can be
done. She went at the dress, and the vizier went
to the Department of Finance, and levied a fresh tax
to meet the expense that he was aware his plan would
involve, making the tax twice as large as would be

required (as was the custom of the country) that he might have the balance for his private purse.

"The next morning he had the dress conveyed to the apartments of the queen.

"'Your Royal Highness holds to your design of becoming an angel this morning?'

"'I do.'

"'Very well. At least go out of the world in a style becoming the sovereign of a great empire. Array yourself in robes such as the Queen of Persia ought to wear. Die in good style, madam.'

"'It is well,' replied the queen, languidly. 'Do with me as you will. In an hour or two I shall be beyond the vanities of this world.'

"And her maids arrayed her in the gorgeous robe and decorated her with the jewels. The work being completed, the grand vizier came in.

"The queen was resplendent; she had got before her grand mirror and was admiring herself. Her eyes sparkled as she looked upon the reflection. The artful dressmaker had so arranged the dress that it made her look not a minute over forty, and a tolerably good-looking woman she was for forty years.

"'The time for your Majesty's sacrifice is at hand,' said the grand vizier.

"'I rather think I will not take the fatal leap to-day,' replied the queen. 'I do not feel well enough.'

"And she stood before the mirror gazing upon herself with undisguised delight.

"The grand vizier saw that he was on the right

track, and seizing the dressmaker by the shoulder, hurried her out of the room.

"'Go to now,' he said, 'make a dress still more gorgeous than this, and have it completed by the morning after this. On your head be it!'

"The next morning the queen put on the dress again, but towards evening, tiring of it, she intimated a desire to go hence the next morning.

"'Very good,' replied the crafty man, 'very good.'

"The next morning he waited upon her Majesty, and with him the dressmaker with the new gown.

"'Put on this gown,' he said, 'and die in it. It becomes your Majesty to die in royal robes.'

"She put it on and stood entranced. So skilfully had the modiste performed her work that she was reduced in age ten years more; she looked not an hour over thirty.

"'Shall I lead your Majesty to the fatal tower?' said the grand vizier.

"The queen settled herself in her skirts and took a long look at herself.

"'No,' said she, 'I will not go to join the angel throng this morning. Heavens! what a dress! I feel in it as though I had been born again!'

"The grand vizier was now sure that he had hit the right idea, and he followed it. He issued orders to the court dressmaker that dresses, each different in design, each more stunning than its predecessor, should be made, and that a fresh one should always be kept in reserve. And whenever the queen got a yearning to go hence, he arrayed her for the sacrifice in a dress made for the purpose, which always took her back to life.

" He did manage to keep her alive by this artifice for three years, and kept his place ; but alas ! the plan was open to the objection of being too expensive. The people growled about the additional taxes, and the grand vizier who levied them was deposed and executed in obedience to the popular demand."

" Well," said the stranger inquiringly, " is that all ? "

" All ! Is it not enough ? Have I not instructed you as to your method ? O stupid man ! Don't you see that to keep your ancient love on earth you must occupy her mind ? What has a rich woman of sixty-three, with nothing on her mind, to do with life ? Life to such people is a burden, and they can hardly be blamed for sacrificing it. Give your lady something to do, and make yourself necessary to her in the doing of it. Get her to start a Society for the Conversion of the Apaches, for the Reforming of the New Jersey Legislature, — for anything, no matter how wild and impracticable, so that she believes in it and gets an interest in it. Then she won't have time to die, for her ' duties' will keep her in life. And then, when she is thoroughly employed, and you have established yourself as a necessity, marry her, and be as happy as you can in the knowledge that if her mania has taken hold strong enough the worry of it will kill her in a year.

" I have said."

And the stranger departed, leaving Abou alone with his thoughts.

XXIII.

THE STORY OF JOBBA, THE AVARICIOUS.

ONE evening the Sage Abou was "wasting," as he expressed it, his time over a newspaper, when, as fate would have it, he stumbled upon an account of a frightful railroad accident, in which a large number of women were injured and several killed outright.

Abou, being in a communicative mood, remarked that it reminded him of an occurrence in his native Persia.

"I will tell it you," he said. "Listen to the story of the wretched Jobba.

"Jobba was a native of Koamud. He yearned for lucre, and was averse to the accumulation of it by manual labor, in which he differed from the narrator of this history.

"There had been a terrible railroad accident in his immediate vicinity, for which, of course, there was nobody to blame. The engineer had wagered cigars with the fireman that he could run the train around a sharp curve, at a speed of forty miles an hour, without going off the track. The engineer tried it and

13

lost the wager, and the fireman was chagrined. The locomotive fell upon the engineer, so there was no hope of ever collecting that bet. He might have asked his widow for it, but he was high-toned, and said he'd rather lose it.

"There were four passengers killed and twenty-three injured more or less. The company was rich. It never spent any money on its track, but it did pay damages to the relatives of the killed and the injured. The president had figured it down to a fine point. He was satisfied that it was cheaper to pay damages than to keep up the road. A great many of the killed had no friends to act for them, and a large number of the wounded never knew that they were entitled to damages.

"But this accident was a serious one. The people on that train were exceptionally influential, and the company was paying rather large damages to a great many of them. Jobba happened to be in the office while this process was going on. One of the victims was a high official from Ispahan, who was on his wedding-tour. He was in a palace-car with his bride when the accident occurred, and the lady had been seriously injured. The car had rolled over twice, had been mashed between two other cars, the stoves had upset and fallen on him and his wife, and they had met with other little troubles, too numerous to mention. His left leg had been broken, also his right arm and two of his ribs, besides which he had been scalped, and one eye knocked out. His wife had not received so many serious injuries, but what she did catch affected her more. A red-hot stove had fallen on her, and spoiled her beauty forever.

"The company settled with this man on the spot. They paid him ten thousand dirhems for his injuries, and twenty thousand dirhems for the damage done his wife.

"Jobba mused for a moment.

"'Sir,' said he to the president, 'do you always pay at this rate for injuries done to a woman?'

"'Certainly,' returned the president, with a groan; 'a jury would give 'em more. It's cheaper to settle than to fight 'em.'

"Jobba relapsed into deep thought. There were three hundred people on that train, and only four were killed. Ten thousand dirhems for the man! twenty thousand for the wife! Four killed, — four out of three hundred. Why, men take greater chances for money than that every day!

"At this point in his reverie another man came in, whose wife was one of the four unlucky deceased, and the company paid over to him twenty-five thousand dirhems.

"This settled Jobba. He put on his hat and left the office, with the exclamation, —

"'I will do it!'

"What was it he had determined to do? Listen, and see.

"Zermina was a venerable maiden lady of not less than forty-two, whose bony frame would not weigh more than ninety pounds. For twenty-six years she had sighed for the 'coming man,' but up to date he had not come. There were wrinkles on her face, there was redness on the tip of her nose, and she had worn a wig for years. She was not beautiful. Had she been beautiful in her youth, and had increased as years rolled on, she would have rivalled Ninon. But she did not start that way.

"To Zermina's astonishment and delight, Jobba called that night, and to her greater delight he proposed to marry her. As she had been waiting and waiting and waiting for twenty-six years for somebody to propose to her, she lost no time in accepting this, her first. She did attempt a little maidenly reserve, but she saw it was wasted on him, and she fell into his arms an over-ripe peach.

"Poor woman! little did she know the fate in store for her! Little did she dream the use this cruel man intended to put her to.

"They were wedded in the morning of a crispy January day, and took the train at Koamud for their bridal tour. Jobba deliberately chose the front seats and entered into conversation with an intelligent brakeman.

"'Many accidents on this road?' asked he.

"'None, sir,' was the reply. 'The rolling stock is A 1, and there is the greatest care exercised by the employees.'

"The countenance of Jobba fell.

"'But we are coming to a road,' continued the man, 'where they have enough of them. On the Jerusalem and Joppa they had had five in a year.'

"Jobba brightened up. They were rapidly ap-

proaching the Jerusalem and Joppa, and to the surprise of Zermina he announced to her a change in his
route.   When they came to the Jerusalem and Joppa
they would take that road and go to Jericho and see
the Falls near that place.

" It was so done, but, strange to say, there was no
accident.   The road was fearfully rough, and as the
cars bounded over the humped and terrible track the
face of the sordid Jobba lighted up with anticipation,
and as they struck the slight and worn rail and went
on in safety, he would relapse into gloom.

" They went the whole length of the Jerusalem and
Joppa line, and. then Jobba announced to his astonished wife that they would go back over it.   He had
lived with her a few days, and felt that an accident
was now a necessity to him.

" ' Why not take another route back, dearest ? '
asked she, with her most ghastly simper.

" ' Why, because — but never mind.   We go back
over the Jerusalem and Joppa.   Ha ! ha ! '

" And they did, but there was no accident to speak
of.   The train got off the track twice, and they ran
over a team or two at crossings, but none of the passengers were injured.

" Then commenced a series of the wildest pilgrim-
ages ever known or dreamed of.   Jobba was a
determined man.   He immediately sent Zermina off
to see her aunt, and selected the worst routes he
could figure from the guide-books.   She came back
scrawnier than ever, but unharmed.   Then he mort-
gaged his farm and put money in his purse, and

started with her himself. He went to India with her over the Ural Mountains; he tried all the new roads that had never been ballasted, and particularly those which permitted drunken employees; he travelled over all the land-grant roads; over all the roads in the mountainous districts of Persia; he lived on the Ispahan road three weeks; he went South on the strap railroads; he became as familiar to conductors and brakemen as any commercial traveller; he became known as the Man with the Wild Eye with the Woman of Supernatural Ugliness. He was perpetually on the railroads, but his presence was a safeguard to a train. No accident that amounted to anything ever happened to any train he was on. He expended all his money in travelling, and then he converted a little estate that Zermina had, and commenced on that.

"But it all availed nothing. He could not find an accident. They would happen on trains before him, and on trains behind him, but never to him. He became the Wandering Jew of Railroads.

"At last his means were all exhausted; he could pay no more fare, and he found himself penniless and with Zermina on his hands.

"'Woman,' he said to her fiercely, 'you have been my ruin! you have been the *ignis fatuus* that has led me to destruction! I shall leave you to-night; you will never see me more!'

"'What have I done, dearest?' said she, bursting into tears.

"'What have you done? You have not been man-

gled ; you have not been crushed ; no stoves have
fallen on you ; you have not had sleeping-cars fall on
you, — in short, you live ! You have disappointed
me. I can collect no damages for you ! '

"And he snatched a watch from her girdle, and
rushed out into the night. The next morning he
pawned the watch, and rushing to the station, demanded a ticket.

"'Where to?' asked the gentlemanly and urbane
agent.

"'Anywhere !' he exclaimed, fiercely, throwing
down a handful of coin.

"The agent gave him a ticket to the end of the
road.

"He took his seat, and glared fiercely at the passengers.

"The train moved on. It was speeding merrily at
a rate of forty miles an hour. As the train shot past
villages, hummed through fields, and rumbled over
bridges, no one supposed that death was ahead of
them. Jobba sat by himself. There was gloom on
his countenance and rage in his heart. He had lived
for an accident, and had met none. Zermina was
alive, and —

"There was a crash. The engine was too heavy
for a rotten bridge that the superintendent had really
intended to have had repaired the year before, and
the train went into a ravine two hundred feet deep.
The *débris* was removed, and under two stoves and a
cattle-car were found the mangled remains of Jobba.
He was very dead — he had found his accident at last.

" How inscrutable are the ways of Providence ! how mysterious are the mandates of Fate ! Zermina sued the company for the death of her husband, promptly, and actually recovered forty thousand dirhems. On the strength of the verdict, one of the jurymen, who had a good farm, married her. The company never paid the verdict; but the husband was a weak man and Zermina was happy.

" Thus the evil intents of wicked men are made to work good. Thus was the instrument designed by the absurdly wicked Jobba to make a fortune out of an innocent though ugly woman made to furnish that woman a weak husband and a home for life. Thus was a wicked engineer hoisted with his own petard, and the old lesson, that honesty is the best policy, once more enforced.

" How rejoiced is the teller of this tale that he is honest and virtuous ! "

" Were there so many railroads in Persia when you left that country as you have enumerated in the story ? " I asked the Sage.

" Is there a moral to the tale ? " was his reply.

" There is," I answered. " Virtue triumphs, as it should in a tale, and vice is ignominiously defeated."

" Then be content without prying into particulars too closely. Be content if the story has a moral and is good. Suppose I had used stage-coaches or camels, instead of railroads, to illustrate my point ! Go to ! "

And the Sage declined to vouchsafe further answer to my query.

XXIV.

TWO OBITUARIES.

A PROMINENT citizen of our village died one day, and I read to Abou ben Adhem the glowing obituary in the village paper which followed his demise.

" If there is a hereafter," said I, " and if the spirits of the departed get hold of the newspapers, how pleased they must be to know the estimation in which they were held by their fellows ! "

" Possibly, and possibly not," replied Abou. " The spirits unfortunately know just how much truth there is in the published obituaries, and how much of them is false, — that is, if the spirits have that increase of means of knowing that is popularly supposed to be given them in lieu of the clay that they abandon when they go hence. That knowledge, I should suppose, would lessen the value of these post-mortem endorsements. I have in my desk an obituary of an acquaintance of mine, published in the Koamud 'Observer,' which I will read, and then an obituary of the same person written by his confidential clerk,

who knew him, which illustrates my point.   Listen.
This is from the ' Observer ' : —

" ' DEATH OF MUSTAPHA, — A GOOD MAN GONE.

" ' Koamud sustained yesterday the severest loss
that has ever befallen it.   At 4 o'clock, P. M., the
immortal part of Mustapha, the general dealer, left its
tenement of clay, and winged its way to the side of
the Prophet.   The disease of which our late lamented
townsman died is yet in doubt.   The medical profession are divided in opinion: one eminent practi-
tioner is firm in the belief that it was pneumonia;
another, acute inflammation of the bowels.   But it
recks little what he died of: he is dead, alas ! and
Koamud is in mourning.

" ' Mustapha was a native of Poska, born of poor
but honest parents.   The opportunities in Poska for
a poor but honest man being limited, he came to
Koamud thirty years ago, determined to win his way
by his own honest efforts.   That he might hew his
own way to distinction without putting himself under
obligation to any one, he rejected the offers of assis-
tance, which, as he often remarked, his honest, manly
face extorted from the citizens of Koamud, and,
nothing better offering, took a contract to cut two
hundred cords of wood for the late Doobla Fesch, who
at the time operated an ashery in connection with
his general store.   We have heard Mustapha narrate
this incident a thousand times.   How his eyes would
sparkle as he narrated the incident and expressed the
pleasure the possession of the first money he had

ever earned gave him! "I had found the road to fortune," he said. "It was to earn money and live within my earnings."

"'His course was after this comparatively easy. Doobla Fesch admired him so much that he took him first as a clerk in his store, then as a partner, and at his death, fifteen years ago, Mustapha succeeded to the entire business, which he so energetically pursued as to leave at his death an estate of not less than a million of dirhems.

"'Mustapha was a public-spirited, kind, generous man. The beautiful pump in the public square was his gift; it was he who paid off the debt of the mosque in which he worshipped; and there are scores of widows and orphans in Koamud who will lament his death. His modesty was as great as his charity. When he made his gifts he insisted upon not being known in connection with them, but his noble clerks admired their principal too much to keep his good deeds shaded by the cloak of modesty he would have kept over them.

"'He was an eminently just man. Careful always to get what was his due, he was just as careful that others should receive their dues. He was a liberal, high-toned, public-spirited gentleman, — one who had no vices, and whose life was so blameless as to make it an example to all about him. As we said, his estate will foot up over one million of dirhems. Peace to his ashes!'

"This is from the Koamud 'Observer,' and it does not vary much from the average obituaries in the pa-

pers on this side of the water.   But there was another
account of the man written which was never published.   It was put upon paper by Mustapha's confidential clerk, in the form of a letter to me.   I will
read it to you that you may see the difference : —

   " ' Old Mustapha's dead, and I 'm glad of it !   A
more solemn humbug, a more cheeky quack, was
never born, or if born, never survived infancy.

   " ' I have known him, man and boy, for thirty years ;
indeed, I was Doobla Fesch's clerk at the time Mustapha cut cord-wood for him, which, by the way, was
the only honest work he ever performed.   He got
about Doobla by cutting a cord or two more than the
contract called for, so that when the wood was meas-
ured he could say, " I was anxious to have enough,
sir."   On the strength of that he got into Doobla's
store, and then his opportunity came.   He stole
enough from the old man in five years to get a partnership.   The old man got into a habit of drinking
the strong waters of the Franks too regularly, which
habit Mustapha carefully encouraged, and finally he
swindled him out of the other half, and had the
whole.

   " ' He run the business *then*, he did.   He bought
damaged goods and sold 'em for first-chop, and there
was n't a trick in the trade that he was n't up to.   He
did n't sand his sugar, for that would have been found
out, but the pailsful of water he poured into the barrels of strong waters was something sublime.   I
caught him at it once, and the old villain had the impudence to tell me he did it in the interest of tem-

perance. "Indulgence in strong drink," he said, "is not only against the law of the Prophet, but it is bad in every way, and if we can so arrange it as to make 'em drink less liquor and more water, we've really served the Prophet. But you need n't mention it to any of our customers, and, Hafiz, bring another bucket of water."

" ' He had a trick of mixing good tea and poor, and when a woman who thought she knew what tea was, came in, he 'd show her some of the best, and say, "Woman, there is a pure Young Hyson at ten kopecks a pound, but here is an article which was sold to me for second-grade which really seems to me to be just as good. I am satisfied it was a mistake in the tea-dealer, and I could sell it for what I believe it to be — first-chop. But I will not take advantage of his error. I sell it for exactly what I bought it — second-grade."

" ' And the woman would take the stuff at nine kopecks, and think she had a bargain.

" ' He was an acute old gentlemen, was Mustapha. He lent Rosten, the goat-skin dresser, one hundred dirhems, and took a mortgage on his house for the amount. Then he made Rosten's family buy all their goods of him, and that was added to the mortgage with interest for a year or two. Interest is about the most hungry animal I know of. Well, Rosten could n't pay, and Mustapha took his house, and Rosten, being old, went into his service at nothing per month but what he could eat, and the family got scattered.

"'The people talked about this so much that Mustapha rushed to Ispahan, and bought a pump for the grand square. It was a naked woman, pouring water out of a pitcher. He set it up at his own expense, and presented it to the people in a letter, in which he said he only lived for the sake of the village in which he had made his fortune. It was dedicated one day with music and speeches and fire-works. From that time on, when any carper would connect Mustapha's name with Rosten's, he was immediately and effectually put down with the remark, "Mustapha a bad man! Look at that pump!"

"'By the way, he wrote a long account of the gift and its importance to the town, and made me copy it and take it to the editor of the "Observer" as my own matter, and made me say that the giver was too modest to let it be known to any extent, but that I loved him so that I would not consent that the good deed should remain a secret. Oh, he knew how to do it!

"'Rosten died, and the memory of the swindle with him, but the pump remains and squirts,—which shows that stone and iron are more lasting in this world than memory. Possibly Mustapha has gone to a world where the memory of his transactions stands longer than the granite he left behind him. I hope so

"'Mustapha's great point was never to depart from his system of doing things. His reputation for honesty was the very apple of his eye, and he worked it always. He had a trick of running out of his shop to correct mistakes, which amused me till it got to be too common to be funny. For instance, an old woman would be buying of me, and I would figure up the amount all right, and make her change all right, and she would load up and start. Just as she was putting her packages on her cutsa, Mustapha would look at the bill I had made, and rush out into the street.

"'"Ten thousand pardons!" he would exclaim, "there is a mistake here. Here are eight kopecks your due. Hafiz charged you a kopeck a yard too much for that cotton. It went down yesterday, and I have been too busy to mark them down, for which negligence may Allah forgive me! It is not Hafiz's fault, O mother! it is mine. I always stand the fall in goods."

"'And the old lady would be pleased, and would tell all her neighbors that Mustapha was the honestest dealer in the country.

"'Then he would make an error of the kopecks against himself, and rush out to collect it.

"'"You may think it small and mean, Father Zamor," he would say, "in me, to insist on the kopecks, — I who give away thousands a year in good works; but it is business. If the mistake had been in my favor I should have been just as urgent to have it corrected. Accuracy, my dear sir, and fair, square dealing are the guiding stars of my existence. Thank you. Hafiz, enter these kopecks and change the footings accordingly."

"'And Zamor would go away and say, "Mustapha is

close, but he's safe and square. One knows what he's about when he deals with old Mus."

" 'He married twenty-five thousand dirhems with his wife, who was a widow with one child, and he worried the life out of the widow and drove the child away from home. But he put up a splendid monument to the memory of his " beloved wife," and wept bitter tears over the obduracy of the girl who would persist in leaving his protection. But she never got a kopeck of her mother's money.

" 'It was funny to see him subscribe ten dirhems to a charity, and then turn and charge two dirhems each to ten careless customers who run accounts and never examined the bills. Why, I have known him to do it a hundred times; and he always took precious good care that the subscription lists were published.

" 'In short, Mustapha was a hypocrite, a swindler, and as dishonest an old villain as ever lived or died. I stayed with him all these years because I had nothing else to do, but I am glad he is gone, no matter who succeeds him. It cannot be any worse.'

"My son," said Abou, as he concluded reading the paper he held, "this statement of the character of Mustapha was, as I said, by a man who knew him, and you see the statement made by the newspaper differs from it somewhat. Which is the nearest correct you may judge; but this advice please take: So live that when you die your body-servant will speak good of you. You may trust the newspapers and the tombstone makers: what you want is the good opinion of those who are nearer to you, and who, having no interest, can speak the truth. This is all. The man that a dead man should be afraid of is the one who stands behind the curtain with him. The public only see him when the curtain is rung up and he is dressed for his play. Go to !"

14

XXV.

THE FIDELITY OF ZAMORA.

LAST Monday, early in the morning, a young man from a neighboring village came to Abou ben Adhem to know what he should do in a matter that was wearing his very soul out of him.

"State your case, my son, state your case. The physician doth not diagnose before he sees the patient, except the advertising mesmerists, who are, to use a phrase of ancient Persia, frauds. State your case, and be brief, for life is short."

The young man did state his case. It appeared that he loved a young woman, and was to have married her; but having lost his property, her father refused his consent and the affair was broken off.

"Now, *I* can bear it," said the young man, "but Hannah Mariar will die of grief. She loved me, and does love me, desperately. She wrote verses to me. Here, listen, I will read them to you."

"Pause, rash young man!" said Abou, with a fiendish glare in his eyes, as he deliberately cocked his shot-gun. "Venture so much as the one line,

'Like a sun at morn is my love,'

And you die! I can endure much, but none of that."

" But how shall I comfort Hannah Mariar, and save her ? " implored the young man.

" Listen," replied Abou. " Once I was young, and I had a Hannah Maria ; only, as it was in Persia, her name was Zamora. Oh, how I loved that damsel! By night I dreamed of her and by day I thought of her. I neglected my business to dance attendance upon her ; I scaled walls, on the top of which were spikes, to see her. I did everything that a foolish young man ever did, for her sake.

" And she loved me madly and devotedly. She was wont to say that if cruel Fate should separate us, if only for a month, she would fade and die as does the lily in the heat of the ardent sun ; she would grow pale and wan and so on, and would gradually descend into the silent tomb. And she would lay her beautiful head upon my breast, and repeat a poem she had written for me, the first four lines whereof were these : —

> " ' I live — I exist in thee, love !
>   To me thou art honey and wine.
>   The voice of the bulbul or dove
>   Is not sweeter to me, love, than thine.'

" There were thirty more verses, in which I was compared to everything that is grand, graceful, sweet, beautiful, and lovely on earth below and in heaven above.

" Well, one day the Shah wanted troops, and I was enrolled — what you would call drafted. I was in great distress. *I* could endure the separation for a year, but I knew that Zamora would die, because she said so, with her head upon my breast, and her sweet eyes, filled with tears, looking up into mine. I could not endure the thought.

" I hied me immediately to a famous magician in Koamud, — this was before I went into the business, — and told him my troubles.

" He laughed a harsh and discordant laugh.

" 'She will die of grief at your absence, will she? They generally do. Young man,' said he, turning fiercely upon me, ' would you know the future?'

" ' I would,' I replied, ' for it can only reassure me, and satisfy me of Zamora's truth.'

" ' Have you two dollars and a half — that is, I should say, two dirhems and a half about your person?'

" ' I have.'

" ' Give them to me, and behold! Three months hence.'

" I looked upon a screen that was at the farther extremity of the room. There came upon it, first, some indistinct shadows, which grew more and more distinct, till finally they took permanent shape. What did I see? It was Zamora, *my* Zamora, and with his head on her breast was Zamroud, the bellows-mender, he looking up into her eyes, and she looking down into his.

" ' Dost love me, Zamora?' murmured Zamroud. ' Dost love thy slave?'

" ' Love thee, Zamroud?' answered the girl, her eyes filling with tears, through which passion shone

with double lustre, 'love thee? Listen to a poem I
wrote this morning for thee. It is the simple reflex
of my feelings. Listen:

> ' I live — I exist in thee, love!
>   To me thou art honey and wine.
>   The voice of the bulbul or dove
>   Is not sweeter to me, love, than thine.'

" And she went on with the thirty other verses,
and ended by kissing him and swearing eternal fidel-
ity, and that, should anything separate them, the
cold and silent tomb would claim her a willing victim
in six months.

"'Wouldst see more?' demanded the magician
of me.

"'I would,' was my reply.

"'Two dirhems this time. Look! Six months
hence. Zamroud is gone to the wars.'

Again the screen filled with two figures : one was
Zamora, the other Osman, the camel-driver. He
lay with his head upon her breast, his eyes looking
up into hers, and hers looking down into his.

"'Dost love me, Zamora? Dost love me?' murmured Osman.

"'Love thee, lord of my life! love thee? Listen
to a poem that I wrote this morn, inscribed to thee.
I wrote it down because it is the reflex of my own
feelings and the best expression of my love. Listen,
Osman, delight of my soul! Listen!

> ' I live — I exist in thee, love!
>   To me thou art honey and wine.
>   The voice of the bulbul or dove
>   Is not sweeter to me, love, than thine.'

" And she held that unfortunate youth in her arms till she had poured over him the other thirty verses, and they parted with sweet kisses, she swearing that if fate should part them for even six weeks the cold and silent tomb would claim her a willing victim.

" ' Wouldst take another handspring into the future, young man?' asked the magician.

" ' I would. I will take one more whirl at it,' was my reply.

" ' One dirhem and a half,' promptly replied the magician.

" I antied, as we say in the East, and the screen was once more illuminated.

" ' Nine months hence,' said the magician. ' Osman has been drafted and has gone. Look !'

" The figures on the screen took shape again. It was Zamora, as before, but with her, this time, was Hakoa, the armorer.

" ' Dost love me?' sighed Hakoa, with his head on her breast and his eyes looking up into hers.

" ' Love thee? love thee? Great Allah ! I love thee as never woman loved man. Thou art my first love ; I never loved before ! Listen, Hakao, to a poem I wrote this morning for thee, which reflects my feelings as the silver stream reflects the moon. Listen, darling, listen !

> ' I live— I exist in thee, love !
>   To me thou art honey and wine.
> The voice of the bulbul or dove
>   Is not sweeter to me, love, than thine.

> ' Do I love thee?' —

" I did not stay to hear the other thirty verses, for they had got to be somewhat monotonous. With a howl of anguish I rushed from the room, and went away to the wars somewhat easier in my mind as to what would happen to Zamora.

"Need I continue this tale? The magician had shown me truly. The girl did have all those three on her string within nine months, and at the beginning of the twelfth month she married Bugo, the rich shawl-seller, to whom I hope she is still reciting the thirty-one verses that she made such good use of.

"And this perfidy to me, who was serving my country as commissary's clerk!

"Young man, go thy ways in peace. Never mind her. As extreme piety is in many cases simply aggravated dyspepsia, so love is, in many more, tight-lacing, unhealthy rooms, rich food, and French novels. She will recover in a week, and her appetite will come back to her as good as new. She will be in love with another man in three weeks, and you will have passed out of her life as completely and entirely as though you had never been in it.

"And reverse the case and the results would be the same. Go. I am weary."

And the young man departed, and Abou went into his laboratory and resumed his experiments.

XXVI.

THE AMATEUR DRAMA IN PHŒNIXVILLE.

HAPPENING to mention one morning to Abou ben Adhem that the young gentlemen and ladies of the village were organizing a Dramatic Association, and speaking in commendatory terms of the project, the sage remarked that it would dissolve in less than a week.

"Why?" I asked. "There is dramatic talent among our people. Give it opportunity, room for development, and who knows what may happen?"

"That's the trouble," replied Abou. "There's too much talent. Listen to the history of a Dramatic Association which I knew of in Maine."

"Were you ever in Maine?" I asked, with an expression of surprise.

"My son, I have been in many places. But listen.

"There was a Thespian Society in Phœnixville which was organized by a number of youths who felt within them the burning of the flame of genius in a histrionic way. Each one, from Simeon Tippetts, the barber's young man, up to Adolphus Pettibone, the son of the village lawyer, felt that he had within him genius that only needed an opportunity to show itself, to entirely eclipse the triumphs of the greatest of the world's stage-heroes.

" A travelling theatre had given a series of ' Theatrical Representations' in the hall of the village. Mr. Herbert De Lancy, ' of the New York Theatres,' and Miss Virginie Adalina de Montagu, ' of the principal theatres of England,' had filled the *rôles* of Macbeth and Lady Macbeth, Romeo and Juliet, and Hamlet and Ophelia, to the intense admiration of the villagers, such as attended. It is true, the company reaped nothing but glory in Phœnixville ; for to get out of the village they were compelled to pawn a portion of their wardrobe and scenery, and (for the credit of free America I dislike to say it) Herbert de Lancy, the Macbeth of the previous evening, was compelled to walk, absolutely walk, through the mud to the next town for the want of the paltry two dollars and a half which would have paid his fare on the railroad. He did it cheerfully, for, as he gayly remarked, he was not encumbered with baggage. His trunk was a bandanna handkerchief.

" ' What of it ? ' said he. ' 'T was ever thus. Homer begged his bread from city to city. The wor-r-ld will yet acknowledge Herbert de Lancy, and Phœnixville will yet blush.'

" The performances, or rather ' classic renditions,' of this troupe set the young people of Phœnixville in a fever of histrionic excitement. With the pawned scenery of the Herbert de Lancy company as a basis, twelve young men, with four ladies, organized the Forest and Macready Thespian Society, — of which Adolphus Pettibone was made President, and Simeon Tippetts, the barber's man, Secretary and Treasurer,— and determined to go at once into rehearsal for the purpose of affording Phœnixville rational amusement and themselves improvement in dramatic literature, each 'gentleman member' contributing two dollars as an entrance-fee.

"Adolphus Pettibone was a short, puffy youth, of nineteen, four feet nine in height, with bowed legs, and weighing perhaps one hundred and ninety pounds. Simeon Tippetts was a young man of perhaps the same age, an inch or two more in height, not much thicker than a candle, and with knock-knees. There were ten other young men of various styles. Of the young ladies, the eldest was Miss Aurelia Mason, the village milliner, who confessed to twenty-seven cold winters.

"Miss Aurelia was popularly supposed to have a great deal of genius in her, based upon the fact that she had read and could quote the most of Tupper's 'Proverbial Philosophy,' and Adolphus Pettibone and Simeon Tippetts also believed that they had been endowed with the divine spark.

"The Society met the night after the organization to decide upon the play they should produce on the opening night.

"There was but little trouble in this, for the Herbert de Lancy combination had played Macbeth on their last night, and the glories of Macbeth were

still in their minds. Adolphus Pettibone preferred
Hamlet, but he was not particular. Macbeth was
accordingly selected as their first play.

" The next business in order was to cast the play,
that is to say, distribute the parts among the members.

" Simeon Tippetts rose at this point to make a
few remarks. What he wanted was no jealousy.
There were different degrees of talent; the members
could n't all play the best parts, and in the minor
parts every one should take the part assigned him or
her, without murmuring or hesitation.

" 'Of course,' said Simeon, 'I shall play Macbeth.'

" Immediately the other eleven rose to their feet,
and exclaimed, '*You* play Macbeth! Ha! ha! A
tallow candle in Macbeth! Ha! ha!'

" 'You mean you will play second murderer,' said
Adolphus Pettibone. '*I* shall play Macbeth.'

" '*You* play Macbeth!' shouted the other eleven.
'Ha! ha! *you* Macbeth! With your shape! Non-
sense!'

" And remarks were made likening him to a tub,
to a Berkshire pig, and to other objects, animate and
inanimate, that were thick and heavy. These allu-
sions to Adolphus' figure aroused his ire, and he
retorted by alluding to Simeon as a candle half-
dipped, as a lightning-rod, a billiard-cue, and other
thin things.

" 'Well,' said Miss Aurelia Mason, 'I hope you
will decide quickly as to who shall play Macbeth, for

it will be necessary to read with him, if I play Lady Macbeth.'

"Immediately the three other lady members of the Forest-Macready Thespian Society sprang to their feet, with the remark in chorus, —

"'*You* play Lady Macbeth! *You* play Lady Macbeth! Ha! ha! ha! te-he!'

"And they made remarks touching her, the point to every one of them being that no matter who should be selected to sustain that character, *she* should not be the party.

"One bright young man, Seth Bagshot, took in the situation and thought he saw a way out of it.

"'There is,' said Bagshot, 'but one principal male character, and but one principal female character. We men of the Society cannot all play Macbeth, nor can all the ladies play Lady Macbeth. Let the matter be decided by ballot. Let the twelve gentlemen vote their preferences for Macbeth, and the ladies for Lady Macbeth, and let that vote be final.'

"This suggestion was adopted, and the vote was taken. Alas for poor humanity! Every one of the twelve men received just one vote for Macbeth, and the handwriting on the ballots betrayed the awkward fact that every individual man had voted for his individual self. And when the ladies' ballots were counted out, it was found that each lady had voted for herself for Lady Macbeth!

"The trouble with the Society was, there was too much talent in it. Adolphus Pettibone resigned indignantly, then Aurelia Mason did likewise, and

before the words Jack Robinson could be pronounced, fifteen of the sixteen had resigned. Simeon
Tippetts was about to resign when he fortunately remembered that he was treasurer as well as secretary,
and that he had in his possession twenty-two dollars
of their money.

"'Give me my two dollars,' quoth Adolphus.

"'I have no authority to pay out the Society's
money except upon bills that have been properly
audited,' quoth Simeon.

"'Give me my two dollars!' yelled the distressed
eleven in chorus.

"'Gentlemen,' said Simeon, 'I am the treasurer
of the Forest-Macready Thespian Society, and will
pay money, on the order of the officers, to any one
having bills against the Society? Have you bills
against the Society? No? Then why this demand
for two dollars? Go to!'

"'I will sign an order for my two dollars, as president of the Society,' quoth Adolphus Pettibone.

"'*You* sign an order! *You* president! Why,
you resigned and are not even a member of the Society. I am the only member of the Society. I have n't
resigned, nor do I intend to. I propose to keep
alive the love of the drama in Phœnixville. Go to!'

"And Simeon went out with the money in his
pocket, and there is a legend in Phœnixville of a
wild orgie that he held, in which all the wild young
men of that village participated, except the eleven,
and that the next day, while the fumes of the liquor
he had drank were still in his brain, he was asking

every one to join the Forest-Macready Thespian Society, and vowing that he was going into the business
of organizing Thespian Societies, as the best thing he
could do.

" The Society was never reorganized, and Phœnixville never was delighted with its home talent.

" Adolphus Pettibone subsided into law, Simeon
Tippetts still shaves, and Aurelia Mason still makes
and trims bonnets ; but all of them firmly believe
that if they had had half a chance, there would be
new stars now shining in the theatrical firmament,
and they all are sorry for the world.

"What happened in Phœnixville will happen here.
Armies of generals are very popular, and could be
easily raised by volunteering, but it takes drafts to
fill in the private soldiers.

" There are enough who will gladly play Macbeth
gratuitously, but it takes necessity to get in the
people to play the parts that have no glory in them.

" There is a great moral in this, but you must find
it yourself.   I am too weary to point it out to you.
Go !   I would be alone."

I thought I saw the moral, so I did not press him
to dwell upon it.

XXVII.

THE STRUGGLE OF KODOSH.

"CAN there be any combination of circumstances that would justify a man in selling his soul to the Evil One?" asked a hoary-headed citizen of Abou ben Adhem.

"My venerable friend, the short story of Kodosh of Koamud will answer your query. But let me preface my narrative with an expression of opinion. I never believed that the Evil One ever bought any souls, that is, by making specific contracts for them and promising specific things for them. Unless his dominions are more roomy than I suppose them to be, he gets more people than he can accommodate, who come to him of their own accord. But this is merely an opinion. He may have more room than I have any idea of, and men may dodge him, finally, better than I think.

"But this is the story of Kodosh of Koamud.

"Kodosh was a worker of burgoos, and was utterly and entirely worthless. He would work only when he could get nothing to eat in any other way, and as for his family, be chesm! he paid no more attention to them than as if they were not. Lusta, the wife of his bosom, supported the six ragged children that had been born to them, by washing for other families, and to get bread for them she never had the time on her hands to do her own. Consequently, dirt, rags, vermin, and disease abounded in the hut of Kodosh perpetually. The master of this house spent his whole time in public places, where the dissolute meet to squander their time in idle conversation, — the time which Allah gives us for the improvement of ourselves and those about us. He knew all the places, which in Persia are known as ‘dives,’ where the strong waters of the Franks are dealt out and where the intoxicating opium is smoked.

"And that was not all of it : he had a habit of coming home full of strong waters, which craze men, and then he made things very uncomfortable for Lusta his wife, and the little furniture in the house. He thought nothing of breaking a stool over her head, which was followed invariably by smashing all the crockery. As this happened almost every day, life was not a rose-tinted dream to the poor Lusta and her children. In fact, one of the children was kept constantly on the look-out, and when he would yell, 'Dad's a comin'!' (Dad is Persian for father), they would all scatter and hide till after he fell into a slumber. He was less disagreeable when asleep than at any other time, for then only his breath was offensive.

" One day Kodosh awoke from a drunken slumber

in great distress, and he called vociferously for
Lusta. She came and found him blue with terror,
and his teeth chattering like the castanets of the
dancing girls who amuse the Shah when he is
weary.

" ' What 's the matter with you, you beast? ' asked
Lusta. ' Has Allah at last taken pity on me by
smiting you with an incurable disease? Or have you
done me the only good possible by taking poison?
Don't crush my rising hopes by saying that you propose to live.'

" ' Neither, my dear, neither,' was Kodosh's reply ;
' but I am in sore trouble.'

" ' I have been thus, O son of the Evil One! for
twenty years, that being the exact time I have been
thy wife.'

" ' But I am in dire trouble. Listen, O wife of my
bosom! While I slept, after my — labor — the Evil
One came to me in person ; he had his tail on, his
hoofs, and likewise his horns, and — '

" ' Miserable Satan that he is! Why did he not
whisk thee off with him? ' ejaculated Lusta.

" ' Listen,' said Kodosh. ' The Evil One wanted
me. He offered me all that I could eat of the best,
and drink of the best, and wear of the best for
twenty years, and all the wealth I wanted and all
that you could desire, if at the end of that period I
would become his, soul and body.'

" ' And what answer did you give him? ' asked
Lusta, anxiously.

" ' I did not give him a definite answer. I said I
15

would ask you and be guided by you, at which he smiled a sardonic smile, and saying that that would answer, disappeared. Now Lusta, love, what shall I do?'

"'Do!' replied Lusta, 'do! O idiot! there was but one thing to do. Why did you not close with him at once? Oh, sudden opportunity, possibly lost forever! Oh, blessed chance, possibly no chance at all! How do you know, son of a she-ass, that he will ever come to thee again? Twenty years of good food, clothing, and plenty of money, for thy worthless body and still more worthless soul! O mush-brained imbecile! long before twenty years have rolled around thy body will have been destroyed by spontaneous combustion, and as for thy soul, that is the Devil's already. He has a first mortgage on it now. Had he consulted his bookkeeper and discovered how you stood with him, he never would have made you so preposterous an offer. Oh, why did n't you close with him? He was swindling himself out of whatever he proposed to give you. You could well afford to close with him for ten dirhems, for one dirhem, for anything. O idiot! O imbecile! This is too much — too much!' and she wept bitterly.

"Of course the Devil never came to make the trade, for Kodosh only saw him in an incipient fit of *delirium tremens*.

"But Lusta's answer furnishes a proper answer to your question.

"If a Devil were to come into the world to-day, and offer wealth and honors and things of that nature for souls, and should take souls as they run, he would very soon go into bankruptcy; for he would be paying for his own property. Most people approached by him should lose no time in closing the trade. Then what a terrible per cent is there whose souls are too small to be worth the offers the Devil is credited with making!

" To me the case is clear. If the Devil ever comes to you with an offer of anything in particular, accept it at once. By the time you have got rich, served two terms in the Legislature, gone through two elections for Senator, and tried to go to Congress, you may be tolerably sure that the Devil will get you in the end, and if you can get any price for yourself now, make no mistake, but take it.

"You are answered, let me rest."

And the Sage went in and laid him down with what he said was the Koran.

XXVIII.

THE DISAPPEARANCE OF THE SAGE.

IMPORTANT business kept the editor of these pages from visiting his " philosopher, friend, and guide " for two days after the interview last recorded. Very early the third morning did I turn my steps towards his dwelling, hoping to hear more from his lips of that wisdom which for a year had been to me sweeter than the honeycomb and more strengthening than the flesh of kids.

To my sorrow he was not in his house. There was no smoke ascending from his chimney, the doors of the house were locked, and the place had a desolate, abandoned look which appalled me.

" Where are you, my friend? " I cried; but the only answer was the echo which mocked me.

While going about the dwelling to find some way of effecting an entrance, a carriage approached, from which four men alighted.

They were singular appearing men, of a style that I had never seen before.

"Are you Abou ben Adhem?" demanded one, seizing me by the collar.

"Bah!" said another, "let him go. That idiot is not the man we are after."

I stood as a man distraught. I did not like the rough handling; the application to me of the word "idiot" hurt me more; but the fact that my friend was not only gone, but that he was sought for by such men, pained me more than all.

"Indeed," I replied, "I am not Abou ben Adhem. Would that I were that great and good man! Can you tell me, gentle sirs, where I can find him?"

"That is what we would give something handsome to know ourselves," replied the first speaker. "The cuss got wind of our coming for him, and has cut his lucky. But we will find what he has left behind."

And without any ceremony he broke down the front door of the house, and going through the sitting-room to the door of the sacred laboratory, he applied his sacrilegious foot to that, and entered with as little ceremony as I would use in entering the barroom of the Eagle Hotel.

"I was shocked at the way in which they ransacked that room. The stuffed alligator was thrown down and kicked to pieces; the owl was treated in the same manner; and the skulls and thigh-bones with which the room was garnished were kicked about as though they were footballs.

"But when they came to the furnace they became intensely interested. They threw down the back arch, and under it, in a cunningly-constructed receptacle, they found many sets of dies, which I regret to say were of the coin of the country, and none of them above the denomination of five cents.

"Taking these things with them they went away, leaving me alone.

"I opened Abou's desk and found everything in it in confusion, as though the occupant had decamped in great haste, and had not had time to arrange his matters properly. From papers left behind him, mostly letters, I discovered how grievously I had been imposed upon.

"It was not Abou ben Adhem who had occupied this house and this room, nor a Persian sage, nor a Persian at all. The real name of the imposter was Zephaniah Scudder, and he was a native of the State of Maine. There in his desk I found a wig of long white hair, and a false beard of the same material, and on the floor were his robe of black, his leathern belt, and his slippers. I read letters that revealed the history of the man.

"All that a cursory perusal of a few letters a year before (which I mentioned in the preface to this volume) indicated, these letters confirmed. He had been everything by turns (except an honest man), and nothing long. He had taught dancing, singing, writing; he had been a horse-tamer, a veterinary surgeon, a dentist, a showman, a politician, an editor in a small way; he had preached, practised medicine, speculated in lands, and in everything else; he had married wives in a dozen places; in short, he had done everything that was disreputable or semi-disreputable, and had finally embarked in counterfeiting the smallest coin, but two, that our Government makes.

One note hurriedly written on wrapping-paper accounted for his hasty departure. It read thus : —

" Get out quick. The cops will be onto you to-morrer."

His accomplices (for of course he had confederates) were never discovered, and he was never seen in the place again.

I was deceived in him, but I do not feel that his residence here was altogether without use to me. True, I would like to get back the five hundred dollars I lent him, and I would be better pleased if I had not intrusted one thousand dollars to him to invest in railroad stocks, since I have learned that the certificates he gave me were forgeries ; but, after all, I benefited by him and do not complain. Wisdom is better than money, and wisdom I received of him without stint. I am, however, sorry for those who lent him money without getting wisdom ; their experience must be their compensation.

" He has gone from my gaze like a beautiful dream." I have his wig, his beard, his robe, his belt, and his words. I am not wholly bereft.

THE EDITOR.

JANUARY, 1875.

"A Charming Romance of Girlhood."

SEVEN DAUGHTERS

By Miss A. M. DOUGLAS.

AUTHOR OF "STEPHEN DANE," SYDNIE ADRIANCE," "CLAUDIA," "KATHIE STORIES," &c., &c.

One Vol. 16mo.　　　　　Illustrated.　　　　　Price, $1.50.

• • • "The spirit of the book is admirable." — *Transcript, Portland.*

• • • "A natural, vivacious, pure story, one of Miss Douglas's best efforts." *Methodist, N. Y.*

• • • "We can heartily commend it as unexceptional in its teachings and tendencies." — *The Christian World, N. Y.*

• • • "A very charming and lively book, the sale of which will be large, for it deserves it." — *The Standard, Syracuse.*

• • • "The book is bright, fresh, and unhackneyed, and gives some pleasant domestic pictures." — *Advance, Chicago.*

• • • "No one who reads faithfully to the end, can help being won by the easy naturalness with which the story is told." — *Commercial Bulletin, Boston.*

• • • "This story is one of the truest pictures of home life, as it should be, that we have ever read." — *Christian Era, Boston.*

• • • "Of our modern writers of fiction we know of none whose purpose is purer, or whose books can be more confidently submitted to young girls, than Miss Douglas's." — *Boston Journal.*

• • • "Very fresh and pleasant reading, with touches of gentle satire and quiet humor." — *Christian Intelligencer, N. Y.*

LEE & SHEPARD, Publishers, Boston.

LEE, SHEPARD & DILLINGHAM, New York.

Mr. Caudle Speaks.

FIRESIDE SAINTS.

Mr. Caudle's Breakfast Talk,

AND OTHER PAPERS.

COMPILED BY J. E. BABSON.

One Vol. 16mo.   Uniform with "Wishing-Cap Papers."   Price, $1.50.

. . . "An array of Douglas Jerrold's irony, sarcasm, wit, and humor, that will be welcome to his admirers." — *Commercial Bulletin, Boston.*

. . . "It is singular that so large a number of such delightful papers, by that most genial jester, Douglas Jerrold, should have lain so long unbound." — *The Times, Chicago.*

. . . "The sketches in this book are quite diverse in character, but all made pleasant by that subtle vein of humor, that quaint fancy, and that easy and graceful style, which lent such a charm to all of Douglas Jerrold's works." — *Golden Age, New York.*

. . . "None of the papers in this volume are included in the collected works of the author, and will therefore be read with keen delight." — *Advertiser, Portland.*

. . . "These essays, though many of them so brief and light as to be properly denominated thumb-nail sketches, merit preservation with the other writings of this spicy and pungent author." — *Post, Chicago.*

. . . " Everybody knows Douglas Jerrold — he of the caustic humor and biting wit ; he who could write as sweetly and sunny as the most genial, and at the same time could wield the arrows of satire as could no other English writer." — *Keystone, Philadelphia.*

LEE & SHEPARD, Publishers, Boston.
LEE, SHEPARD & DILLINGHAM, New York.